Ghost Cartel

James Marquis

I0538601

GHOST CARTELL

James Marquis

Copyright © 2021 by Madeline Zech Ruiz,
madrzech@gmail.com

Hardback ISBN 978-1-952114-57-1
eBook ISBN 978-1-952114-58-8

eBook available wherever digital books are sold.

All rights reserved. No portion of this book may be repro-
duced, stored in a retrieval system, or transmitted in any
form or by any means – electronic, mechanical, photocopy,
recording, scanning, or other – except for brief quotations
in critical reviews or articles, without the prior written per-
mission of the publisher.

Cover Design: Aleksandar Petrovic, vajsman@gmail.com

Graphic Design: Goran Skakic, www.tamigo.co

Printed in the United States of America

Story Told by Lucifer

"Ghost Cartel"

Lucifer saved King's life when he was
twelve years of age.
Since then, King pledged his support
to Lucifer
for the remainder of his life.

CONTENTS

"Ghost Cartel"
is dedicated to
"ANTONY"

$\mathcal{A}$s the author, people have asked me why the characters for this book are from Kenya, Africa. That story began with a cocktail party one Friday night in my apartment in Sacramento, California. One of my guests for the evening, built Safari lodges in some of the exclusive regions in Kenya and Tanzania. I found the information so fascinating that I investigated which areas in Africa are the most liberal as to the gay lifestyle. My research revealed Kenya. To validate my research, I contacted Karin, a travel expert specializing in African safaris. I explained my quest to her, and she suggested that I seek out a gay Kenyan man to assist me. My next challenge was to find a person in Kenya skilled in English composition and creative writing. Their task would be to research and write about six gay Kenya couples with characteristics that I could adapt for my book.

Antony was selected out of many others to conduct the research. He interviewed many Kenyan men and putting together, let's say, the leg, arm, head, and body from many to form one man to add to another, creating fictional Kenyan gay couples. It was an amazing adventure for Antony as he had never done this before. He was given 60 days to complete his task. He met the challenge head-on, accomplished it on time, and was highly compensated for the work.

Antony was born in the tribal region of Baringo, Kenya, known for the Lake Baringo Game Reserve. He had two sisters and a brother, and he was the older of the siblings. His father always recognized him as a free spirit in the African world, not focused on cattle and farming like most tribal people are. He enjoyed growing up barefooted playing with his friends in the jungles. When Antony reached 15, he was circumcised at the tribal ritual that all people his age attend. As he said, this is then his attraction for Kenya men began.

Living in Kenya, it is not so easy to catch the eye of another man. Gays live in the shadow and underground, but they blossom and show their creativity for their fellow man when they are giving the opportunity. I was very fortunate to find Antony, who took this project from inception to completion and created outstanding examples of gay Kenyan men.

After a months of Skype calls back and forth, the characters were finished, and I wrote my book. I have so enjoyed getting to know Antony, who has the brightest smile and the warmest heart.

James Marquis
Author

FROM THE PREVIOUS BOOK:
REVENGE BY THE MARQUIS CARTEL

"Jim's internal pain was overshadowing his sexual pleasure. He slowly got up and went to the medicine cabinet to retrieve more morphine, to kill the pain, yet hoping to increase the joy of King's touch. Momentarily, a tingle of numb pleasure overshadowed Jim. King's Jamaican body was thrusting in and out of him with immense delight. As he heard King's moaning, the entire sensation felt unbelievably orgasmic. King kept thrusting to release his final load. Just then, Jim grabbed King around the neck and held his head in both hands and looked him in the eyes. All he could see in the depth of those beautiful brown eyes were a reflection of himself. As Jim was watching his reflection growing dimmer and dimmer, he cried out King's name and grabbed him harder around the neck to bring him closer for one final thrust. As King unloaded what some people would say was his last shot, Jim was numb from the volume of morphine tablets he had just consumed that afternoon and evening. He didn't feel King's quantum amount of man-juice as it buried itself within his lifeless body.

Immediately recognizing Jim's total relaxed state, King held Jim harder and harder as Jim's body became still as he laid on top of him. King knew the feeling of death and now accepted Jim's final breath as his last voyage home.

King whispered into Jim's ear after he shot his final load, *"Now Lucifer will tell our story."*

THE FUEL DOCK

*A*fter Captain Oliver docked the Tito V for refueling at one of the many islands surrounding the Kingdom of Tonga, King stepped off the yacht at the refueling station and observed two handsome African men busily servicing the yacht.

They were so tall and handsome that he could not resist inviting them for dinner that night on board the "ghost ship." "Assir" and "Jaali" were surprised by the invitation. When they arrived at the "ghost ship," at the appointed time, King introduced them to David. King inquired as to how they had traveled from Kenya to the South Pacific. Both were very forthright in mentioning they were bodyguards for the wealthiest person in Nairobi, who respected them and was aware of their relationship. They always lived in constant fear because they knew that the laws of Kenya were against them. For their personal protection, they received assistance from their wealthy friend, who help them board passage on a cargo ship that docked in New Zealand. Having little money, they traveled by night on small boats from island to island until they reached the island of Vava'u in the Kingdom of Tonga. They eventually gained employment at the fuel dock where we met today.

King inquired as to how long they had known one another. They replied since they were children. They had grown up together in the village of Kiambu and had worked in its capital city of Nairobi. After saving their employer's life, on numerous occasions, he helped them to escape to a life of freedom and love in the South Pacific.

David was so impressed by their handsome features that he just sat back in his chair in the dining room, put his hands behind his head, and gazed at their characterized Kenya faces. David said, "The Lords are with us that King could find such a charming couple at the fuel dock."

Assir *(captivating and fascinating personality*)* and Jaali *(powerful*)* were also taken aback by the stunning beauty of the Tito V, the 250' "ghost ship." They were now waiting to be served an elegant dinner prepared by Chef Jeffrey in its main dining room.

King asked, "What type of security do you provide for their employer? You do not appear to be very strong, nor do you look masculine."

Jaali was the first to speak up, "Don't let our appearance fool you. Assir and I have been together for almost a lifetime. During that time, we have been professionally groomed in the art of assassination and personal protection."

"Is there a company you work for?"

Jaali simply replied, "Yes."

They concluded their delicious dinner of lamb and sweet potatoes with fried green bananas with caramel sauce for dessert. Chef Jeffrey outdid himself once again. King, David, Jaali and Assir were just sitting in the luxurious main salon, enjoying after-dinner drinks, when King asked, "Have you ever toured a yacht?"

"No."

"Follow me, boys…"

THE QUESTION

King toured Assir and Jaali throughout the "ghost ship's" many levels and lavishly decorated rooms and teak decks with well-appointed furnishings. Along the way, they were introduced to several members of the crew and staff that live on board. When King reached his master stateroom, he opened the door and invited them in. As the African couple entered his room, in all its grandeur, they looked at one another as if they had just entered the presidential suite of the hotel of their former employer. That was more than equaled by the grandeur of the Tito V floating in the South Pacific.

King asked Assir and Jaali to have a seat in the living area of the master state room and asked if they would like a cocktail or a beverage before they started their discussion. Somewhat nervously, they declined and asked King, "What business are you in to afford such luxury?"

"It's not of your concern what I do; I am more concerned about what you did in Nairobi. What security company did you work for?"

Assir replied, "LL Security Services, and we were both assigned to the Executive Services division. We provided security for diplomats and commercial clients in high-risk and complex environments. Many of our clients were celebrities, people of wealth, and those subject to physical attack or kidnapping.

King's next question was, "How would you like to work for David and me?"

They looked at one another in disbelief. Jaali asked, "What is it you would like us to do?"

King replied, "*The question* was, do you want to work for us or not? It is a simple *yes or no* answer."

Jaali and Assir got up and walked across the massive state room and huddled in one corner. They put their arms around each other and heads touching, began a discussion that lasted less than a minute. They were both smiling as they were walking back to the sofa, and before they even reached it, Jaali spoke up in a loud voice and said, "Yes, we would love to work for you. You name it, I'm sure that we are trained to take care of it."

"That is exactly the answer I wanted to hear. Now, I seal all my business with a handshake and a kiss."

All three stood up extended their arms for that special handshake that led them to the king-size bed. King so delicately kissed their beautiful lips to seal the deal and create the *"black magic"* that was going to now begin forming the "Ghost of Cartel." Despite King's age of over 50 years, his Jamaican body was ravaged by both the Kenya men. Their savage lean body attacks were most welcome. He had longed needed to be re-energized back to his old cutthroat self. Tonight, it is being injected deep into his inner soul.

FORMATION
OF THE "GHOST CARTEL"

The following morning King summoned Simon to the office on the upper deck of the "ghost ship." When Simon arrived, he gave him Assir and Jaali's names and former addresses in Nairobi for GYS to run a security background check. After Simon left, he and David discussed the plans they needed to build a new South Pacific operation. King explained to David that their network of cartel members is maxed out in the Caribbean operation.

King went on to explain, "It is now time for us to build an entirely new team of cutthroat cartel members. We can then control as much of the South Pacific Islands as we so desire. We did a physical security check of our friends from Kenya last night, and they passed with flying colors. They want to work for us and provide us with their experience in Executive Service.

David researched the firm that they were previously employed with and found it to be the best security firm in Nairobi."

Shortly, Simon returned with his report from GYS Security. Assir and Jaali's report came back A+. They had exquisite training and a flawless record, but they disappeared without a trace. They were assigned as personal security agents for the wealthiest person in Nairobi or, in fact, Kenya. Their employer's name will NEVER be mentioned by his former security team or this cartel. They saved his life on several occasions and his gratitude is not one to be questioned. No one knows where Assir or Jaali went. It appears they disappeared from the face of the earth.

After breakfast, Assir & Jaali walked into their spacious VIP state room, shut the door, locked it out of habit, then ran toward the bed. They stripped down to their tall structures of African beauty and interlocked. Throwing themselves on the bed in a passionate heat of desire, they immediately were savoring the strong scent of their man odor, which only exaggerated the sexuality of the moment. They wanted it all, nothing to be left behind. Jaali, the powerful one, grabbed Assir by the ankles and drug him to the end of the bed. As he crawled slowly, with his manhood dragging on Assir's chest, he buried deep Nairobi kisses in his mouth and lifted his legs into the air. Jaali had been preparing for this moment for a long time. He had loved Assir for years, and Jaali's feelings were likewise. So tonight, their mutual pleasure is to seal the deal on their new cartel.

David said, "King, let's call them up to the man cave and start a serious discussion with them on what they have to contribute to our "new cartel."

"That's a good idea, David."

King made a phone call to Wayne, Captain Oliver's first mate, to round up their friends from Africa. When Jaali and Assir arrived, they looked like they had been in a fight. Could it have been the luxury of the five-star yacht that they enjoyed with splendid lovemaking instead of fighting? King summoned Chef Jeffrey to take the breakfast order and then told everyone to enjoy a cup of coffee until breakfast was served.

King opened casually, "How many gay couples are there on your Executive Service detail?"

Assir replied, "The majority of all teamed units are gay couples. Part of our training is that if one team member dies, the other is just signed to another partner, and your service goes on. It is difficult to be paired with a straight individual that is not your soulmate or lover because they will not take a bullet to save your life. You cannot trust a person in our line of work if they don't love you.

The breakfast order arrived, and King was quietly digesting this statement that Assir had just made about survival. He then asked Jaali, "If I asked you to hire five more gay couples from the Executive Service detail in Kenya, can you and Assir achieve this task? If so, how long would it take you?"

There was a long moment of silence. Jaali and Assir again got up and walked across the room to discuss the question. Then they asked the steward for a refill on their coffee and then sat down at the table. Jaali spoke up and said, "Yes, and we could probably get many more. There are many security companies in Kenya, and all of them have an Executive Service detail. Currently, we are the most famous people in Nairobi or Kenya because we just disappeared without a trace. We were known as the bodyguards to the wealthiest person in Kenya. Our network is your network.

NEW LIEUTENANTS

*K*ing leaned back in his chair and finished his last sip of coffee, looked in the eyes of "his ghosts." Now, without them knowing, they are the new leaders of the yet-to-be-established "Ghost Cartel."

King asked, "What will be your action plan to move all of these new members from Kenya? Just remember, I need to pre-approve all new members."

Assir and Jaali went to work. They enlisted Jeff and George's support, longtime crewmembers, who knew technology and communication. By using their networking systems, and their support, they identified 10 couples. Their information was given to GYS security to run background checks. Within 10 days, after Assir & Jaali's interviews, begin the list had narrowed to 5 couples. Four of the couples on the list were personal friends of Assir and Jaali. They had trained, served, and slept with them during their eight years of service. These incredibly handsome men could not even be described as killers. King's review of their portfolios revealed men that could pass as executives, models, very dark-toned workers, and the sexiest men in the world. As King was reviewing the portfolios, his thought was of crafting the new cartel. His members in Jamaica were handsome. He and David will put together a "Ghost Cartel" that no one could ever imagine.

David called Andrew at the Tonga office and told him to have Captain John bring Tito VI along with his partner Stephen to the island of Pangai so that he and King could meet with them. We have some planning to do; we need your input, and we need to utilize some living space on the Tito VI. Captain Oliver notified King that the Tito VI is scheduled to arrive tomorrow morning at 9 AM. Stephen and Andrew arrived at the man cave at approximately 10 AM. King and David had not seen them for several months. They both looked through King's eyes as a young and loving couple on a honeymoon. They greeted King and David with affection and sat down at the table to have the steward request their breakfast order.

King said, "In a few minutes, I'm going to introduce you to Assir and Jaali, two new members of my personal detail. They are exceptional individuals who are lovers and may be instrumental in helping us form a new cartel in the South Pacific. It is time to break away from the Marquis Cartel command and develop our own independent operation. Aaron and Bryan have their hands full with the Caribbean operation; it is growing daily. They have already been contacted and informed that effective immediately, David and I will take command of the South Pacific.

Assir and Jaali arrived at the man cave just as breakfast was being served. Everyone was introduced and proceeded to enjoy the breakfasts. Smalltalk flowed around the table to establish some type of border in each respective relationship. Assir and Jaali were so handsome that the eyes of the table were glued upon them. Finally, they all chuckled and apologized for their glaring eyes.

"It's not often that we enjoy such delicious eye candy."

Assir and Jaali just giggled and acted a little bit embarrassed. After breakfast was finished, David stood up and said, "King and I have a plan. Our new "Ghost

Cartel" will be made up of individuals like you, Assir and Jaali, trained in executive service, that will be undetectable in the cartel world.

Captain John invited Assir and Jaali for a tour of the Tito VI before it departed for the capital of Tonga. It was a complete duplicate of its sister, the Tito V, but at 100', smaller. They noted that Captain John's crew were not as polished and sophisticated as those on Captain Oliver's yacht, but its furnishings were as lavish. In fact, Assir and Jaali even felt slightly threatened by the crew. When Captain John got to his master stateroom, he pushed them in, shut the door, and whispered hurriedly.

"I need your help; the ship's crew had overtaken the yacht. They're forming their own cartel and are attempting to take over King's business. There just waiting for the right time to kill King and David. Do something, you guys, fake your way out of here and go back to your yacht and tell King, he will know what to do."

Assir and Jaali used their "black magic" and made their way off the yacht and reaching the Tito V, out of breath and yelling for the first deckhand insight. Once on board, they told the deckhand that they needed to talk to King immediately; it was very important.

King, dressed in his bathrobe and slippers, made a swift appearance.

"What's so important?"

Jaali replied, "Captain John told us that the Tito VI has been overtaken by its crew members. Your gang in Tonga intends to take over your operation, and they plan to kill you and David."

"Jaali, thank you so much for getting this to me, Will you and Assir ready your skills? You're now in Executive Service for David and me."

King sounded the alarm on the yacht for everybody to report to their assigned stations. Simons rushed to the man cave, and plans were in motion to retake the Tonga office. A big concern was what did Stephen and Andrew know about this mutiny? It was only that morning they were on board the ghost ship for breakfast.

The personnel on board the ghost ship trained for a war totaled 16. That's including King and David. Adding Assir and Jaali to that roster, it now totals 18. King remembered the operation in Tonga was originally staffed by 11 of his members from Jamaica and Andrew and Stephen. Unless they had increased their staffing, they were looking at 13 in Tonga. They also had two "go boats" docked ready to be deployed.

King circled the table in the man cave like the "Knights of the Roundtable." Circling it was David, Assir, Jaali and Simon -- his new "Ghost Cartel."

King said, "Planning for this mission has to be very detailed because surprise is our only weapon."

Simon pointed out, "The office is located on the 300' pier that the firm had constructed. The yacht and two "fast boats" that are tied up there all the time. I suggest that we entice the Tito VI to leave port and get it out in the ocean in a pre-determined location. Ensure that it is fully staffed with its entire crew, then coordinate an attack."

King brought up that the yacht was a significant asset and can be considered "The Ghost Ship II." Jaali suggested that he and Assir slip into town, in their new ghost uniforms (nobility), and interact with the most important people, to find out who controls the dock. The plan was approved.

THE MUTINY

$\mathcal{A}$ssir and Jaali went down to their stateroom and crawled on the bed. They tossed many ideas back and forth on how to approach the Tonga operation. Their final conclusion was to be outfitted as before in Nairobi and mingle only with the wealthiest. The master plan is to charter the Tito VI, during which the ghost cartel would take command. The plan was presented to the King and the Roundtable.

"Ingenious!" said King. "We will charter the yacht, and the ghosts will round up a polished group of individuals that will co-mingle with our team, and at a particular latitude and longitude, the war will begin.

Assir and Jaali spent little time networking the financial center clubs and bars with pockets full of money provided by King. After three evenings, they invited two couples to dinner on the ghost ship. King and David were excited to see the type of individuals their new Executive Service team would interact with.

Before we continue on, Assir and Jaali's physical description, I don't believe, has been thoroughly engraved upon your mind. It's challenging to describe their beauty in words. Lucifer (Me) will attempt to paint a picture. So here goes his verbal description of each as best of my recollection.

1. Assir. Closely cropped hair, with a long jawline. The color of darkened milk chocolate and standing 6"3". His neck cavity is surrounded by a strong shoulder supported by a narrow waist. So passionate to the sight and so loving to the touch. Assir beauty has surpassed his peer's handsomeness so often that he enjoys the control he possesses. The effectiveness of his service to his charge is undisputed, as he can complete all tasks and walk away into the crowd undetected under the darkness of night.

2. Jaali. The mid-back dreadlocks, perfectly braided, covered his muscled 6'4" dark black frame and six-pack chest. His hands were so elegant that they represent a well-educated man. He was built to represent the nobility of Kenyan men, and yet his style of assassination is quiet, swift, and just.

The overall sexuality of a Kenyan man is
not of concern for their partner's sexual orientation
but rather the depth of emotion
love and passion during
moments of intimacy
on the hunt.

By James Marquis

Assir and Jaali will rent the yacht as Kenya royalty. Simon will be their personal bodyguard. All of the fighting crew of the Tito V will be combined with the new members to supplement the cartel. They will now total 17, thus outnumbering the crew of the Tito VI. All were armed with silent weapons; they were trained to make one shot a kill and move on to the next. Two days later, when the Tito VI had docked back at the Tonga office, Assir called Captain Oliver to inquire if he could charter the yacht. Andrew, the office manager, always looking to make a quick buck, told Captain Oliver to have the call transferred to his line.

Negotiations for the charter were quite detailed. Assir was quite demanding as to the service level that his guests expect. They are all wealthy individuals who desire the highest in service. A preference sheet was faxed to Andrew as to the specifications for the five-day charter. The cost of $1,000,000 per day was not a hesitation—50% due upon boarding, with the remainder due at the end of the cruise. Andrew and Stephen were slapping each other on the back for making such a large amount of money, in such a short time, without doing anything illegal or committing a crime.

Andrew informed Captain Oliver to call a meeting on the dock. When the crew members were gathered, Andrew told them, "The yacht has been chartered by royalty from Kenya for a five-day cruise. They will require the highest of service while onboard. Anyone's failure to provide the highest in service will be fired or eliminated in some way."

Stephen confirmed with them that they understood their charge, and Captain Oliver was given the chartered locations that they had plotted for their course.

Going over the last details with Simon, King remembered that Aaron and Bryan had dispatched Dakota from their cartel operation in the Caribbean to Tonga during its inception. King contacted Stephen in the Tonga office and ask what duties were assigned to Dakota? Stephen replied that he was their dock foreman, and all of the crew on the dock and yacht report to him. The red light went off in King's head. The culprit behind the rebellion was "Dakota." He had squirmed his way into Stephen and Andrew's bed to keep them sexually occupied while he formed the new cartel.

There was only one flaw in their plan. Assir and Jaali had both been on the Tito VI. After using their "black magic," they vanished into the night. When they boarded with their entourage of killers, they needed to be disguised in their tribal royalty attire. As nobility from Kenya, the dress is exquisite. Black robes to below the ankle with an African print neck scarf surrounding their face with a crown of thatched weavings tilted on their head. There was absolutely no suspicion whatsoever when all the staterooms were now filled with the "Ghost "Cartel." They stood ready to take back their yacht and terminate the Tonga operation.

Over dinners and drinks, they assessed their plot, joining together for one last drink on the stern of the yacht. The self-service bar was fully stocked. The crew had been released for the remainder of the night. It was now time for King and the Roundtable to finalize the strike. Nearing the latitude and longitude preprogrammed for the hit, another set of adventurers were hired to take the "go boats" to within 10 miles of the desired location and wait. The radar on the chartered yacht would not recognize the "go boats "as an active threat. Once King's attack is underway, a signal will be sent to the "go boats" to head their way. Assir and Jaali are so perfectly trained that they could out 8 good people without a strain.

The strike was to begin when all were on the back deck. Each member of the charter party would request some "special" personal service from a crew member. When each crew member is engaged in servicing a "ghost," that is when the unexpected arrived. The crew was eliminated one and a time. Some were thrown overboard, and some were left for dead on the deck. Then they were cast off to float among their comrades in the middle of the South Pacific. Within two minutes of the strike, all but two of the former crew members were left on board. A few others, alive and dead, were bobbing around in the water, waiting for the "go boats" to arrive. One remaining surviving member of the cartel, whose name was not known, kneeled before King, a totally guilty man. King had been to his secret room onboard and retrieved his gold-plated machete. Displaying King's lack of mercy, he executed that man. Throwing his head, then his arms and legs overboard to charm the sharks, and his remains would disappear for eternity. The only person left on board was Dakota, who had been with King and his organization for years. He reported to the leaders of the Caribbean operation.

Dakota was transferred to the Tito V. His fate would be determined by Aaron and Bryan, Kings trusted lieutenants on Marquis Island and charged with the Caribbean operation. King put a call in on the secure line to the island, Aaron answered, and the conversation detailed the problem at hand. Aaron was in disbelief that Dakota would turn his back on him and Bryan. They had been together for almost a decade, committing such crimes. Aaron's reply to King's question was, "Cut off his tongue and release him on a deserted island in the South Pacific. Death would be too good of an honor for him."

POST ANALYSIS OF THE MUTINY

*K*ing and David sat at the head of the roundtable and looked at Assir and Jaali with admiring eyes. They had put together and accomplished one of the most sophisticated and swift cartel missions that either one of them had experienced. David was so excited that he even got off the first shot.

King stood up with all of his 5'9" Jamaican structure and told Assir and Jaali, "You two are the new leaders of the "Ghost Cartel."

David went on to say, "You have been our leaders from the beginning. We just needed you to execute the plan, without position or title, to demonstrate the teamwork you have with our group."

Assir and Jaali were proud of themselves for achieving such a position. With their training in executive service and the trust their former employer told the world about them, their reputation was now starting to proceed them. King asked them about the two couples that they had employed from Tonga. Assir explained that they caught the couple doing a drug deal in one of the ritzy clubs in the financial district. It was pretty apparent that their client was of wealth. After his transaction Jaali approached one of them by the bar. He invited them to join them at their private table in the secluded part of the club.

"Why?" was his immediate reply.

"I saw your deal," Jaali said, "I think you can join us, and we can negotiate a buy."

Kaelo and Abayi follow them to their secluded table. Assir introduced Jaali and instructed the waiter to bring them a cocktail for them to enjoy. Smalltalk started the conversation, leading to compliments in looks and adornments. The guys from Tonga inquired as to Assir and Jaali's heritage as they appeared to be from a foreign land. They explained there from Kenya in the continent of Africa, and they had enjoyed the South Pacific since their arrival two years ago.

Kaelo and Abayi were taken back by their beauty and grace. These two gentlemen weren't merely handsome; their features were those of ancestral charm that history books write about. Here before them in royalty are two perfect pages out of history.

Jaali asked, "How long have you been dealing the white powder?"

"Several years."

"What type of arrangement do you have with your clients, may I ask,' Assir said.

Kaelo was the first to respond in very general terms. "Our operation is high class and low-key. We are an outcall drug service for the very wealthy. And that's our only clientele."

Jaali said, "You know all of the wealthy people in the capital of Tonga and the surrounding islands, is that correct?"

"Yes."

"How are your skills in protecting yourself?"

"We are not challenged by others. Kaelo and I have been together for years and have developed the keen art of survival, taught to us by our mentor. We did start at the top for a local drug network. We have a long history together; would you like to hear?"

David said, "Most definitely."

"Abayi and I grew up in the slums on one of the remote islands. At the age of 12, we took a canoe and rowed to the island of Neiafu. We were living on the streets when we met a very polished and sophisticated English man who took us in and raised us as his sons.

His lifestyle was so intriguing that we favored it for ourselves. He taught us how to survive in a cruel world, not only with a smile but with a knife. His friends were well established among the wealthy by which we were also befriended. The rich enjoyed the fascination with drugs during their weekly events.

"Through our mentor's network, we were connected to the highest level of the Tonga drug cartel. We were supplied with the best product to sell to our wealthy clientele. When our beloved English man died, he left us more than his entire estate. We were left with the entire white powder distribution operation for the wealthiest of the Kingdom of Tonga."

The next day Abayi and Kaelo were asked to come on board the Tito V to meet with King.

Jaali said, "You sure proved your worth to us yesterday. Would you like to continue the relationship?"

Kaelo and Abayi looked at one another, and Abayi said, "What's in it for us?"

"King and David are putting together a new team in a South Pacific. As part of our private security team, you would also live aboard the Tito V and be afforded all of its luxuries."

Kaelo said, "How about Faitua and Siaosi that joined us on the operation? We have known them for some time. They are straight. They were both married at one time, but now they're currently divorced. They live together, and we know nothing of their personal lives except they have extraordinary talent in carrying out missions such as we executed yesterday."

Jaali said, "I'll follow up with them tomorrow."

"If you get them to join the team, we're all in."

"Jaali," King said, "give me your phone number, and I will give you a call tomorrow.

FAIYUA AND SIAOSI

The next day King called the phone number that Kaelo had provided. Faiyua answered the phone. King immediately thanked him both for the services that he and his partner had delivered on the mutiny operation and asked if they would like to join him and David for dinner on the Tito V at 7 PM.? There was a brief pause on the phone while Faitua consulted with his partner, and they both agreed to the dinner invitation.

Siaosi and Faitua arrived 40 minutes late. King and David were in the main salon waiting for them. David mentioned to King that's this was not a good way to start off our dinner meeting. He thought that Chef Jeffrey had everything already prepared. When their guests arrived, the chief steward guided them to the main salon and requested their drink orders. King told the steward to bring the drinks to the dining room because they were already running behind schedule.

The first thing that David mentioned was, "It appears that Kaelo paid you handsomely for your services in support of our mutiny operation."

Siaosi said, "Yes, he knows the quality of our services. They don't come cheap. This is quite an impressive vessel. May I ask what business affords such luxury?"

David replied, "Our business in the Caribbean was very successful, and King and I have been retired for almost 2 years. Retirement has been challenging for us, and we are now looking to form an "executive service" business in the South Pacific.

The chief steward served dinner with the utmost efficiency. King and David observed their guests eating their meal as if they were sitting in some pub in the poor part of town. Obviously, they were skilled in the art of killing, but they were not polished enough to be members of their executive service detail.

Faitua spoke up and said, "This dinner is delicious. Do you guys eat this way every day? "Yes."

Siaosi said, "Kaelo told us you two were both gay, and in fact, the entire crew of the yacht was gay. We're both uncomfortable around that lifestyle, but the bottom line is that money is what's important to us."

Just as they were finishing dinner while coffee was being served, Kaelo and Abayi walked into the dining room. Everyone got up and shook hands and then took a seat around the massive dining room table. Abayi was the first to speak up and said, "First of all, Kaelo and I want to thank you so much for your outstanding support in our mutiny operation. King and David has offered both of us a position on their new "executive service" detail that they are forming in the South Pacific. We were thinking of joining if you would join along with us. It would be reassuring to have someone from Tonga to cover our back."

King broke in, "You never have to worry about your back being covered in our operation. Everyone on the Tito V or VI are family, and if they're not, you just experience what happens to them if they try to double-cross you."

Faitua looked at Siaosi and said, "Count us out. We don't want to float around in the South Pacific on a yacht filled with faggots. What in the hell are we supposed to do for entertainment? We don't suck cock or fuck guys. We are for hire, though, for special assignments. If you need us, just call us."

They thanked David and King for the delightful dinner and drinks, departing the yacht and disappearing into the Tonga night.

THE PLAN

$\mathcal{T}$he vacationing crew that used to be on Tito V has been transferred to Tito VI to supplement its staff members that were executed during the mutiny operation. Five VIP Staterooms are now empty, which will accommodate ten new crew members. Assir and Jaali have already been assigned a VIP stateroom as the new leaders of the "Ghost Cartel."

David, King, Assir, Jaali and Simon sat in the mancave and began to formulate the plan for their new South Pacific operation.

King began, "I see five couples trained in executive service, all from Kenya, that will be personally selected by Assir and Jaali. They will be dispatched to the major islands in the South Pacific that David will choose. The ultimate plan is to control the high-end narcotics suppliers. The concept that I envision is like the historical story of Robin Hood. Robbing from the rich dealers and selling at a lower price to the small dealers on all islands in the South Pacific.

Assir and Jaali thought they'd better get busy using their network to identify qualified candidates to join the executive service detail. David started his research of the most identifiable islands for incoming drug shipments. King negotiated a deal with Kaelo and Abayi to remain on board the Tito V and enjoy all the luxuries that the yacht offers for three months. Then they could decide if they want to continue working in the newly formed "executive service" detail.

That night while King was relaxing alone in his master suite, there was a knock on his door. When he opened it, there stood David. He stood with the biggest smile. Dressed in his sexy yacht attire, tight white pants, boat shoes with no socks, and his shirt open to the navel. His blonde hair flowed loosely over his brow, and his hands were always soft to the touch. There was this slight callous on his second finger on his right hand from doing so much writing and paperwork. But other than that, he was a perfect specimen of a man that God could ever create.

"What is the pleasure of this surprise visit?"

"We have not had any private time together for several weeks. I thought we could share a few drinks, laughs and hugs while we're in the planning stages for our new "Ghost Cartel." One never knows what tomorrow brings; we are both aware of that."

David laid his head on King's shoulder. At the same time, King put his arm on David's shoulder and kissed him on the forehead. They sat there in momentary silence, enjoying each other's love and companionship. David always felt safe with King. Despite the fact, David stood 2 inches taller, but his sixpack was not there. David was the brains behind the financial end in the business and did not possess King's cutthroat tactics or strength. That tonight while David curled up next to him in that king-size bed, King thought back on the many nights that he and Jim had made love in this very same bed onboard the "ghost ship" of the Marquis cartel.

Assir and Jaali both used the secure line to contact the new executive service detail used by his previous employer in Nairobi. Their replacements were shocked to hear from them but so pleased that they were alive. They put forth their request in total confidentiality and asked them to further network it through their trusted friends within the security firms in Kenya. They gave them a complete description of the candidates' requirements and a fax number to submit an application.

The next day with David's uncanny way of discovery, he started to identify the most important islands that would reveal the biggest incoming drug shipments in the South Pacific. The search had to follow large shipments from Australia and West Africa. These two mega exporters of drugs use the South Pacific islands as drop-off locations in transit to their final destination. When King asked David what progress he was making, David shared with King that the large shipments are very well hidden, and he will have to dig deeper into the web.

IAN AND CYPRIAN

*A*ssir and Jaali got their first fax from Kenya. One of their networks faxed the names of Ian and Cyprian, who work for a small G4T security firm located in the city of Eldoret. They were excited to get their first candidate for security services for their new cartel. Assir gave the names to Simon to perform his standard security background check.

King reviewed the portfolios that were sent via fax. Both Ian and Cyprian are of Pokomo culture, having grown up together in a small village in the Simot Forest area of Kenya. When Simon returned with the security review results, it revealed that they had been very effective on their various assignments. Every client has given them high ratings on their personality, looks and communication skills. Their employers emphasized in each performance evaluation how impressed they were with their polished protection skills, which most tribal people from this area cannot perform.

King called Assir and Jaali to the man cave.

"First, I like to congratulate you both on finding excellent candidates for your security service. It didn't take you more than four days to get this done. Amazing job. Let's arrange for Ian and Cyprian to fly to New Zealand. Then they can take a helicopter to the Tito V wherever we may be at the time of their arrival."

Assir and Jaali were again honored by King and David's accolades as the new "Ghost Cartel" leaders.

David made the travel arrangements for Ian and Cyprian from Nairobi to New Zealand. Upon their arrival in Wellington, New Zealand's capital, a helicopter would be waiting to transport them to the Tito V. Prior to their arrival from Africa, Assir and Jaali remembered their interview with King. "All deals are made with a handshake and a kiss." If the interview goes well and they are approved and accepted a position in executive service for their new cartel, King, will close the deal with a handshake and a kiss, as the great cartel leader always does.

Two days later, Ian and Cyprian arrived on the Tito V via helicopter from New Zealand. King was standing on the bridge of the ghost ship, watching as both men walked across the yacht. He instantly noticed that they were relaxed individuals in tan slacks, button-down long sleeve shirts, and were African black. As the crew on the yacht approached them to welcome them on board, they could see these handsome men had smiles that would stop any heart from beating without knowing why. Simon escorted them to the man cave where the ghosts of the roundtable were there for them to meet. David, King, Simon, Assir, and Jaali all stood up, shook hands and welcomed them aboard the 250' ghost ship, now navigating the waters off of Auckland, New Zealand.

"Your handsome qualities certainly complement your resume of work," King said. "I hope that our questions will be answered to their fullest if you desire employment in our executive service group. We only employ those with specialized talent both on the street and in the bed chamber where one sleeps. Meaning… no question is off-limits. Are you agreeable to that?"

They both confirmed by a mutual nod, and Ian said, "Begin with your questions; we have nothing to hide. We have the talent and training to be in executive service from the jungles of Africa to the street of the bustling city of Nairobi to your bed in the South Pacific.

Jaali asked the first question. "How long have you been lovers, and when did your first sexual encounter begin"?

Ian, being more the aggressive one, replied, "We have been childhood buddies for a very long time. We had to keep our love between one another a "secret." Being gay in the Pokomo culture is an abomination. As we grew up, our love flourished under the cover of the Simot Forest, where we herded cattle together during the school holidays. Cyprian and I have been bonded together for life because we underwent the "cut" (circumcision), sharing the same knife.

King inquired as to how they handle the emotional reality in the assassinations of multiple men. Cyprian responded, "Ian and I know that stakes are much higher than anything that we have faced before, but we faced numerous animal attacks out in the jungle when we were growing up."

Then Cyprian stood up and showed the group his leg with a massive scar from a crocodile attack. Together they fought off the vicious attacks, once killing a crocodile by using their combined strength. The skin of this immense crocodile is used today in tribal ceremonies in their village. Their names are in history and legend, as the conqueror of the beast.

David asked, "Are you interested in working with us in the South Pacific?"

"Ian jumped in and said, "We'll do anything to get out of Kenya and have a life together. Living in the beautiful South Pacific on this most beautiful yacht would be a dream come true. King stood up and asked them if they had ever toured a 250' yacht, and their answer was no.

"Well, then boys, follow me."

HANDSHAKE AND A KISS II

As before, when King gave Assir and Jaali their tour of the yacht, Ian and Cyprian were introduced to crew members and staff along with the many decks and hallways. When King arrived at his master suite, they were asked in. King shook hands with a kiss on the lips and invited them to the large bed in the master suite. Neither objected to this advance because they were excited to explore the body of the king of the cutthroat Jamaican cartel. Ian, the hairier of the two, kissed Cyprian on the cheek to assure him that everything they would do with King was to seal the deal on their new job in the executive service on an island for the ghost cartel.

The three interlocked with such passion that Cyprian was too horny to reciprocate; he lay frozen beneath his lover's body. The kisses began, so he laid lazily, breathing heavily and faster and faster as Ian caressed his slender body. As King sat to watch the two African lovers intertwined, he was fascinated by their tribal lovemaking, as it was genuine.

Soon, Cyprian yelled out, "Ian, Stop."

But Ian was having none of that, his hairy balls touching Cyprian's clean-shaven crotch. Ian pushed his erect penis against Cyprian's belly. Cyprian grabbed Ian by the waist, pulling him closer to him so that Ian could start his manly dominating attack.

King got out of bed, sat in one of the chairs, and observed two tribal natives exploring their sexuality for the first time aboard a yacht. Ian ran his tongue over Cyprian's body all the way down from his neck to his now rigid nipples, then to his hairless balls, which he savored for a long time before he proceeded to his inner thigh. His lips lingered around the scar made from the crocodile's attack when they were swimming in that river many years ago. Ian continued thrusting so many manly moves. Ian's man juice release on Cyprian's chest was so white and thick; Ian reached down and wiped up a hand full so that it could be shared with his lover. King admired their deep passion that he had just witnessed.

Ian and Cyprian lay there looking at the ceiling of the master suite, each one thinking about the decision that they had just made. How were people going to react to them when they were put in charge of all cartel activity on an island somewhere in the South Pacific. Will their love survive the stress of the executive service ahead?

King crawled in bed between them and knew that Cyprian was the passive one and brought him to a climax. King then shared Cyprian's man juice with Ian with a wet kiss, which has just been extracted from Cyprian's long spear. It was so delicious and pleasing to the taste.

They sat naked in the living room of the master suite, each having the opportunity to admire each other's bodies. The fresh young men from Africa were envious of King's 50-year-old Jamaican body, standing 5'9" with 8 inches swinging between his legs. His rumored reputation as a cutthroat killer, leader of the largest cartel in the Caribbean Sea, and a loyal leader along with David, the only leader alive of the original Marquis cartel. King's protection of David goes with a question. Their relationship is never to be challenged by anyone in the organization.

THE ORGANIZATION

David had spent several weeks analyzing the drug activity in South Pacific. He had identified five islands that the most significant shipments of incoming drugs were transported to. Then the drugs were cut and further distributed to various ports and islands throughout the Caribbean, Africa, Asia, and Australia. At the same time, when the islands were identified, new yachts, along with two "go boats" for each location, were being ordered to support their drug activity.

New Zealand – 200'
Fiji – 175'
New Guinea – 175'
Samoa – 150'
New Caledonian – 200'

While David was analyzing operation centers, King had been on the phone with Jake Goldstein, the yacht broker from the Netherlands. All the yachts owned by the Marquis Cartel had been purchased from Jake's company, and King and Jake had an excellent working relationship. He gave him an order for five yachts as described above and 10 "go boats."

"Keep the color and the lines the same as the ghost ship or the Tito V. The new yachts need to be delivered fully staffed with captain and crew and sailed to the ports-of-call yet to be provided. Send the billing for the yachts to my Tonga headquarters; bank drafts will be issued in full payment upon each yacht's delivery."

As the Marquis cartel being a long-time customer, having ordered six new yachts in the past, cash on delivery were terms that Jake would accept.

Ian and Cyprian checked into the 2nd VIP room on the ghost ship. They felt as if they were in heaven. No one could've told him seven years ago, when they were herding cattle in the Simot forest, hiding their love for one another from the world, that today they are accepted as lovers, in a position of authority, in the newly formed "Ghost Cartel" in the South Pacific. They melted into each other's arms; Ian once again took control over the situation. He grabbed Cyprian by his slender waist and twirled them around, and when they came to a stop, he gave him a long kiss. They eyed the bed and decided it was the perfect time to inaugurate their cabin.

Training for their new position in executive service started at 9 AM each morning, six days a week. For the next three months, new members were added along the way. The plan was to have senior members train junior members as they come in. The first batch of inductees should be completed in approximately three weeks, and that's how long it would take to screen new applicants to join the ghosts in training.

Training for executive service is not all assassination techniques. The diplomatic requirements of service are just as important. They are all trained in the most refined techniques for eating, serving, liquors, and related finery that royalty is accustomed to. Their physical appearance was massaged and groomed. Their island assignment was comparable to their physical features. They were taught the country's philosophy and its people to understand why and how decisions may be made.

TONGA HEADQUARTERS

The Tito VI was now safely docked in Nuku'alofa, the capital city of Tonga. Their large office building sits along their 300' dock with the Tito VI and two "go boats" tied up and ready to go. Since the mutiny, their organizational structure changed, making Andrew and Stephen totally accountable for their office. The expansive Tonga control house will be the distribution hub for their products (stolen from the rich). Every bundle of their contraband will cycle in and out of this center. Quick and clean, the plan. They had excellent control over the environment here as respected businessmen in Tonga with several large yachts that come and go all over the South Pacific.

The training during this time was constant. When each couple got back to their state room each night after dinner, neither had any strength left in their soul for fulfilling their sexual desire. Kaelo and Abayi kept a low profile, not knowing what the plan was. The more they were around David and King, they noticed a powerful inclination that they liked black men. Every 3 or 4 weeks, another gay-black couple would join their ranks and go into training, all from Kenya.

Jaali had been thinking about his two comrades from Tonga. He and Assir had not spent any quality time to get to know their fellow Tonga men. Jaali asked Assir, "Would it be all right to invite them to their state room for a drink?"

"Sure, go ahead."

Jaali wasted no time. He opened the door, walked down to the end of the hallway, turned right, and their state room was just ahead. He knocked on their door, and Kaelo opened it. Rather winded, but with a beautiful smile, Jaali extended an invitation to join them for cocktails and hors d'oeuvres, in their stateroom #1, at 6 PM. Kaelo accepted the invitation and assured Jaali that he and his partner would be there.

Kaelo shut the door, turned around, and looked at Abayi with a perplexed smile on his face. "We have just been invited for cocktails and hors d'oeuvres tonight at 6 PM."

Kaelo and Abayi arrived precisely on time. They were both greeted with a big Kenyan hug and smile.

Assir and Jaali's suite was larger than theirs and very well appointed in a soft color of sand. A gold-braided bedcover dressed the bed, and the surrounding curtains revealed just a slight splash of red.

Abayi said, "Who's the bartender here?"

Assir replied, "How rude of us. What would you like to drink?"

Kaelo replied, "We'll take vodka with a splash of tonic."

Jaali said, "I'll have my standard dry martini, thank you."

Kaelo said, "You are both from Kenya and were personally selected by King himself to be the" Ghost Cartel" leaders. What do you have that is so impressive that the King himself would allow you to hold such a position of power and trust within his organization?"

Jaali replied, "I guess you know nothing of a Kenyan man."

Abayi said, "I definitely would like to find out. Why don't the four of us fill up that beautiful king-size bed and share all the manhood that we possess."

African men are tall and thin in body tone, depending on the African tribe. The main attribute the African man always has over men from Tonga is the size of his spear. No matter the length from start to finish,

Tongan men take second place to African in each race. That may be true, but Tonga men have stamina and strength like a Polynesian man. They wrestled around for a couple hours. Finally, each of the four was satisfied and enjoyed the ultimate from each culture, in their four-way pleasure.

Kaelo and Abayi were the only two non-Kenyan potential members of the ghost cartel. They were officially invited to become a member of the tribe tonight. Their initiation ceremony was one of sheer delight.

Kaelo spoke up and said, "There is no way that Abayi and I will ever measure up. The love and the passion and the sheer beauty of the Kenyan man can never be duplicated and one from Tonga or its islands."

Men from Kenya, no matter
the tribal land,
Have empowered within
Love and passion
that all hunters have.

By James Marquis

Since the request for applicants for executive service went out, the fax machine in their office was rattling off of its hinges. The volume of applicants was overwhelming Assir and Jaali. On their next phone call to their Nairobi contacts, they asked them if they would screen all the applications and forward only the ones we should hire. If we hire your applicant, you each get paid a month's salary for your work. Jaali's and my reputation are being spread all over Kenya. We want to keep a lower profile, so please help us out. Their replacements, who will remain nameless for security reasons, agreed to all conditions, and proceeded with their screening of executive service recruits.

MBINGA AND KAIKAI

The next applications that were forwarded to King and David's attention were those of Mbinga and Kalkai. Their pictures showed a tribal man, 6'3" from Kenya and the other 5'9" from Tanzania. They have been in the executive service to the owner of a large fishing fleet. They have been together for several years in the Lake Lolwe region of Kenya.

Mbinga and Kalkai's history was an enjoyable story in itself. Kalkai was from Tanzania and had hitched rides on various boats to the lower Lake region of Kenya, where he was employed for a season on the fishing boat "Electric Eel" to harvest tons of fish. Mbinga had a deep prismatic voice and was of a towering height. The Tasmanian man, Kalkai, covered with sweat, was more inviting than other men that Mbinga had seduced before. Mbinga had always enjoyed his sexual escapades, cruising from man to man in the many ports they stopped on the lake.

Mbinga's preference for men was a lifelong curse, and to find that perfect companion on a fishing boat named the "Electric Eel "is a story for the Kenyan gods to tell.

The challenge in Kenya for a man to find that perfect male mate is challenged by two things: *family value and faith.* Any man who deviates from a woman walks invisible among his peers until eye contact is made. It was that one special day when Mbinga gazed across the ship, and there was Kaikai's half-naked, rippled, and sweaty body. Kalkai stood out as different from other men. Kaikai noticed Mbinga's eye contact, returned his gaze, and the relationship began.

Over several weeks Mbinga and Kalkai found an empty hut on various islands when they were docked for a brief stop. Mbinga being the tribal men, dominated Kaikai with his man juice in every hole that he had. Kaikai had not felt such pleasure since being a young warrior in the jungle on the hunt. He enjoyed being dominated by the one in power, for when he was in Tanzania, he could not show his loving side.

The relationship grew through fantasy and imagination. Mbinga's fascination for Kaikai's smooth feet gave him delight when he smothered his face in his toes and bathed each one separately. He would proceed up his hairless leg and encounter his inner thigh. Kaikai was always waiting openly for his next sexual surprise. They would often talk in bed, how being "different" negatively impacted their childhoods and wished that the world would be less hostile about love. They cuddled and took out their anger at the world by making love and fulfilling their wild fantasies.

Their relationship grew to the point that Mbinga convinced Kalkai to join him in the perspective service detail for his boss, who owned the large fishing fleet. They have been together ever since that day.

Assir and Jaali were impressed with their resume. David arranged for their flight to the ghost ship for the final interview with King. When they arrived by helicopter, Mbinga was the first one out. He reached up, grabbed Kalbi, and helped him out like a gracious nobleman. King, standing on the bridge, glaring out over the deck, couldn't help but notice the build of these two magnificent men. When Simon escorted the couple to the man cave, they were introduced to King and David. They all shook hands. King immediately noticed that around Mbinga's neck was a braided necklace with a medallion that he clutched tightly in his right hand.

"What is the necklace all about, my friend?"

"Kaikai gave it to me as a symbol of the love he has for me."

David began with, "You guys have had an interesting background. You were recommended to us because of your physical appearance. Giving you the ability to blend into one of the cultural islands that we plan to control. It is not necessarily about your assassination skills."

Kaikai said, "In Tanzania, we are at war most of the time. We learned to survive at an early age. Despite our look, we can defend ourselves and survive."

Mbinga added, "We will defend each other to the death, and no environment will we feel threatened in. Put us to the challenge; that's all we ask. If death comes to us, we will have done our best."

King offered them the job and welcomed them aboard. They both accepted in unison, and room assignments were made. David continued their tour of the yacht and introduced them to crew and staff members along the way. As they reached the hallway to check in on room 3, on the port side of the ship, Kaikai opened the door of the third empty Master

Suite. When they had both entered, they stood in awe. Only three days ago, they were on a fishing boat surrounded by sweaty men on Lake Lolwe in Kenya. During their years they have been together, a hot bath was so rare. They ripped off their clothes and ran to the lavish bathroom with a shower the size of a small boat. They turned it on, and all eight jets cleansed their body. The steam and water blasted every hole and crevice reamed out any dirt of their long trip.

When they emerged from the shower, they lotioned up. Their skin was now a citrus shiny black, laying next together on their queen-size bed. Kaikai asked Mbinga the depth of his love; Mbinga turned Kaikai over and rubbed his bubble butt. Mbinga entered Kaikai so deep that both screamed of pleasure and pain. Kaikai, finishing on his back to share his white cream with Mbinga by licking Kiakai's stomach and tasting that Tanzanian's sweet cream.

LANKENUA AND JAMAL

The fax machine never fails us, does it? As it printed out two additional portfolios of handsome warriors from The Mara. Their associates in Nairobi assured them they would be interested in this couple. They had an infamous reputation with the biggest cutthroat group that operated in tribal areas of Kenya.

"Such interesting individuals, David," King said. "Take one of these portfolios, and I will take the other one."

David took the Lankenua's portfolio. He was raised in the tribal area, educated, and returned home to improve his family's quality of life. He was hired by the chief of the tribe for cattle protection. Has served as the game warden with a very low profile and a quiet disposition. He and his partner Jamal go back 10 years.

King's review of Jamal's portfolio revealed, he was born to wealth and lived on the eastern coast of Kenya until he ran inland to escape a pre-arranged marriage. Then he joined the Al-Shabaab terrorist group. It is now known when he joined the group, he had minimal lifesaving skills. I'm sure he must've improved, for us to get our Nairobi partners' recommendation for them to join our cartel. The report confirms that he has partnered with Lankenua for an undisclosed period of time. Their service to the king of the tribe is reported as outstanding, and they can be sent on any assignment without concern.

King invited Lankenua and his partner, Jamal, to join him and David in the game room, for cocktails, at 7 PM. King always seals all deals with a handshake and a kiss, but it will be different tonight. David is along, so one wonders how King's will handle this. The Chief Steward announced Lankenua and Jamal's arrival to David and King. Orders for the cocktail were taken to be delivered on a silver tray. King sat back for a minute to wait to see who would speak first. That is the trick that he learned in the barrio of Puerto Rico. The person who talks first is the leader. Jamal spoke up as to the beauty of the Tito V. He mentioned that their housing for years has been huts on the prairie land in Kenya called the Mara triangle.

Lankenua said, "Many years ago, I used to be a game warden and had a pretty comfortable life. Then one wonderful night, I met Jamal, and it was a bit freaky, to say the least. Two gay Kenya men in the bushes at night, hidden from sight, exploring the love and adventure that has lasted a decade. I went from one side of the badge to the other and back again. I learned to love, respect, honor, and be devoted to my man, which is the highest honor of *"A Kenya Man."*

King asked the big question, "Do you guys want to work for our cartel? Putting your life at risk 24/7. Making so much money, you can't spend it. Sometimes, you live on a 250' luxury yacht with other guys who are gay. We are a family. We live, eat, sometimes we sleep together. We defend one another to the death. We all accomplish our missions 100%. This is the "ghost cartel." Five personally selected couples. Each assigned to a particular island in the South Pacific. David and I would like to know what actual skills you bring to us as our ghost?"

Lankenua took over the conversation. "Jamal and I are natives of Kenya. We are trained to survive in the prairies with wild animals, dangerous tribes of warriors, and reptile beasts. We are also polished to infiltrate cities, large villages, and financial centers. Look at our skin. It shines like the night; it is professionally treated so we can disappear without sight. We understand four languages, and many other foreign languages are based on some form of our known dialects."

King said, "Do you want to be a ghost, or do you want to go home?"

Jamal spoke up immediately, "We are on board. This is an opportunity that Lankenua and I have been waiting for. Now we can be an openly gay couple to our world; we can truly demonstrate our skills and the teamwork that we possess."

"I'm glad you're joining us. You are a very handsome couple, and I'm sure you have some incredible energy between you. I usually close my deals with a handshake and a kiss. But tonight, David and I will excuse ourselves to allow you to enjoy your new master suite."

Lankenua was watching the beautiful sunrise out of the cabin window of the Tito V. The sun was more beautiful than on the Masai Mara, known to the locals as "The Mara" -- the expansive national Park that explodes from the Nile basin. He turned around while he was sitting on the sofa and observed the empty bottles of expensive wine scattered about on the tables in the master suite from the extravagant crew party the night before. He sat there feeling slightly excited and scared at the same time. The excitement was of the forbidden love life he and Jamal have chosen for themselves and the fear of being accepted as a hand of the ghost cartel. All of this happening within days of leaving The Mara.

Over the years, Lankenua was working as a game warden in the Masia Mara Game Reserve. Jamaal came from a well-to-do family from Malindi on the coast of Kenya and could not take the pressure of being something that he couldn't be to please his family. To avoid marriage to a woman which he did not love or desire in any way, he disappeared into the outback of Kenya and joined the infamous Al-Shabaab terrorist group. It was known throughout Kenya as the tribe where all men could take a warrior as a lover if they so choose. Jamal has gravitated towards men since adolescence, and his thirst for male domination was increasing, as did his tall, lean structure.

It was now more than ever that he wished his grandmother were present, to affectionately rub his head and tell him how his name "Lankenua" meant the "lucky one" in his native language. As he was sitting next to his soulmate and lover on the queen-size bed, he tenderly touched his own chest, running his fingers over his erect nipples. He rolled Jamaal over and looked into his wide brown eyes. Lankenua removed Jamal's clothing a piece at a time, exposing a tattoo on his chest. Jamal nibbled on Lankenua's lower lip as he moved his lips down his body to his clean and shaved crotch. Jamal felt his shaft pressing on that wall of the cleansed area. Lankenua whispered those magic words in his ear, "take me." No force was held back, and after several attacks, Lankenua's juices exploded all over his chest. Jamal erupted within Lankenua and immediately laid down on Lankenua's chest, looking like an Oreo with cream oozing out. Tonight, they said, we are the ghost of the cartel.

TONY AND MARC

For the past five years, Tony and Marc have provided executive service to a very wealthy landowner near Moi's Bridge, the second-largest city in the Rift Valley and the capital of Usain Gishu County. Their client, whose land was so vast, contributed to more than 50% of Kenya's wheat production. Since employed, they have been exposed to many property takeovers attempts, attempted kidnappings and hostage situations. They had successfully protected their employer and his personal property on every hostile action. During the past two years, their reputation in and around the capital city of Eldoret was on the lips of all security agencies.

Tony grew up in a small village in the County of Narok, in the Great Rift Valley. Tony's fondest memory was when he was 15 years old and had gone to "tumin."

This is a sacred place where boys go to get circumcised and get educated on their tribal culture from elders as their "cut" heals. He considered this as the best time of his life, and it was the starting point of his sexual fantasies with other men. During this ritual, they were all located far away from women, and he got to see the magnificence of the naked man's body paraded before him. He would fold his "suka" and sit on it as he feasted his eyes on these young warriors going up and down in "tandem," showing off their most recent "cut." During his youthful years, he had to conceal his feelings for another man because the Maasai culture did not condone man to man love, no matter the tribe.

Marc grew up in Marigat, a fishing village just outside the city of Kabarmet, home to Lake Baringo. From an early age, his father would tease him as to his feminine beauty. He was the only child of the third wife of the village chief, who had seven wives. He was a very obedient and handsome boy who helped his mother doing the day-to-day activities. Marc felt no shame that the chores were traditionally meant for girls. Despite his father's opinion of him, he was a fearless hunter. By the age of 10, Marc would go alone into the jungle without fear to fetch firewood and hunt for rabbits with a slingshot. He had come close to death several times, always using his quickness and speed and accuracy of his slingshot. He always held the danger of the jungle at bay. As he grew older, he became more skilled in using a spear and bow and arrow. Using these weapons, he downed larger animals for his family and the village to banquet on.

Tony and Marc met while they were attending boarding school. Tony noticed the sparkle in Marc's eye as they frequently passed in the hallway or walking on campus. One evening Tony asked Marc if he would like to join him for a cup of tea, and Marc's agreed very enthusiastically. It was from this occasion that their relationship grew into a partnership for life. After they both graduated from the University, each earning different degrees, they realized their tribal instincts could be utilized by security companies. During the first year of their employment in executive service, they received extensive training in the art of assassination and other survival techniques. Their training was natural to them because they were both warriors and hunters in the prairies and forests of their lands.

Tony and Marc were quickly promoted from one rank to another due to their exemplary work of providing security to the most prominent businessman in Moi's Bridge. They were employed by LL security services. As a result, Assir and Jaali knew of their reputation and their no-nonsense approach in providing protection and dedication to their employer.

When Assir and Jaali's received the portfolios from their contacts in Nairobi, they immediately recognize their names. Jaali wasted no time in referring their portfolios to King and David. King noted Tony and Marc's tall and lean tribal appearance, along with their track record of protective talents, would be a perfect fit addition to their ghosts. He asked David to arrange for them to fly to the Tito V from their location, in Kenya, as soon as possible.

They were both escorted to the man cave by Simon. When they entered the room, King noticed how relaxed they were. Most of the other new cartel members were somewhat nervous upon their arrival. King looked over to David with his usual fatherly look and said, "It looks like we got a couple who just joined us that are really in love."

David asked Marc, "How long have you and Tony been together? May I ask."

Marc replied, "That's a sad story, must I share?"

King said, "Yes, your past is of interest to David and me."

"I don't like to dwell on my painful past, but after I was circumcised and designated a warrior for my tribe, I would go to the jungle and guard our village against attacks. During this time, I met my first lover, Nash. We were caught having sex in the bush, and he was banished from the village for life. My parents then sent me to boarding school. That's where I met Tony, and our lifelong relationship began.

King spent little time inquiring about their executive service career. Assir and Jaali already knew so much about them and their service in the Moi's Bridge area of Kenya.

Tony, the more aggressive of the two, commented on the beauty of the yacht.

King said, "Would you like to tour the yacht?" They both said yes.

"Follow me, boys…"

Do we need to go into detail about what happened next?

The deal was sealed with a handshake and a kiss. Tony and Marc were initiated as new "ghosts" and checked into the 4th master suite at the end of the long hallway on the 250' yacht. When they opened the door to their master suite, it was almost a duplicate of King's but just a little smaller. They turned around and looked each other in the eye, and Tony told Marc to just stand there and close his eyes. He then kissed Marc on his lips, and then Marc pulled back and started kissing Tony again. This time Marc opened his mouth and stuck his tongue slowly down Tony's throat as far as his tongue could reach. This pleasure, so hidden by the door, was one that neither had enjoyed for such a long time. So well protected in their own room, on a yacht somewhere in the South Pacific.

Tony and Marc had been sexually attracted to each other since the day they met. They've tried every possible act of love during their relationship of years past. They grow fonder and fonder of each other each day when they get up to face its challenges, no matter what they are. They were excited to be welcomed as a new member of the "ghost cartel."

DAVID ACT II

*K*ing, David, Assir and Jaali reviewed the portfolios of the new cartel members that their contacts in Nairobi had forwarded to them. All four of them were satisfied with the selection they had made so far. They only had one more couple to be selected to complete their search to complete their "ghost cartel."

David had done extensive research on the drug movement in and out of the South Pacific. The islands that he had identified in his primary search were used as staging areas to break down large shipments of drugs in smaller amounts to ship out to various locations throughout Africa, Australia, and islands in the South Pacific.

Now it was their cartel's task to apprehend these large shipments discreetly like a ghost. Then they would funnel the drugs into Tonga's operations center, where they will be cut and reshipped at a lower price throughout the remaining cartels. The complete strategy for this massive undertaking was yet to be finalized. King relies heavily upon David's finite skills in detail planning to estimate the massive volumes of drugs that may flow through the system.

Once the final couple are on board, the island assignments will be made. Further training will be completed. And King himself will visit each island to get a handle startup operation and to establish dockage or moorings that are safe and secure for their "ghost ships."

ANTOINE AND ZACHARY
THE FINAL COUPLE

*A*ntoine and Zachary were with the security detail that replaced Assir and Jaali, guarding the richest man in Kenya. They had supplied all of the candidates for the new ghost cartel. They had known Assir and Jaali for many years, and their reputation preceded them. Now it was time to share their desire to join the ghost cartel.

Antoine, his baptismal name (Karanja, tribal name), placed a secure call to King on the "ghost ship." During the conversation, he reminded King that they had only one more position to fill in his detail. He and his partner Zachary, again his baptismal name (Omollo, tribal name), would like to be considered for the position. King replied that he has delegated that responsibility to Assir and Jaali and to direct his call to him. Antoine explained that he and his partner took their position when they left Nairobi. As a result, they have a vested interest in ensuring that the former client is well protected. Assir and Jaali thought that he and Zachary were the best available in Kenya in providing their client's a protection detail.

King said, "I understand. Let me talk to them and see how they feel about considering you for the last position."

Antoine thanked King and hung up. King called the office, and Jaali picked up the telephone. King said, "Why don't you and Assir come over to the man cave? David and I would like to talk to you about the last position to be filled."

When they entered the room, King had Zachary and Antoine's portfolios on his desk. He and David had gone through them in detail, and they had a strong record of service. King asked Jaali what his reservation was about assigning them the last position in the cartel. Again, his concern was for his previous employer.

David chimed in and said, "We have started to look for a new security detail for your old boss. Maybe we can find someone out of the applications that we have on file for our position that would be a perfect fit for the job."

Jaali and Assir remembered the application for Joseph and Zane. These two guys met when they were 10 years old at a soccer camp. They spent eight years together training and developing soccer skills and the skills of love and tenderness between them. When they were 18, they were outed by another team member and kicked out of the "B" league soccer team. During the last years of playing on the team, they had earned a small sum of money, which enabled them to branch out on their own and attend schooling for security detail.

Antoine had grown up on the streets of Nairobi and had excellent survival skills. He was well acquainted with the violence and the turmoil of life as he was an orphan. He had joined a gang at a young age and witnessed the brutal slaying of the third of his associates. After that encounter with death, he used his skill in soccer to attend an elite soccer camp for young men, where he met Zachary. Zachary was tall and all muscles, a striking young man who, from the very beginning, Antoine could not resist feasting his eyes upon. Zachary was raised by his grandmother, and his soccer skills were also outstanding. Once both hit the soccer field together, the game was on.

After they graduated from security detail school, they had two brief assignments with politicians as their personal bodyguards. On both occasions, they had saved their clients from kidnapping and received a substantial reward. Saving these rewards, they were able to advance their living standards in Nairobi, polish their looks and communication techniques. They become sought-after security agents for the highest-profile clients.

On their last assignment, it was a calm, quiet night on December 11th. Antoine was standing on the balcony of the Club Ibiza, a local hotspot for the rich politicians. He and his partner Zachary were at the club to provide security for the wealthiest man in Nairobi. Suddenly gunshots rang out. His immediate thought was that of Zachary and his client. He immediately dropped his cigar and hurried down the stairs through a maze of topless and confused barmaids and dancers. Two more shots were fired, and a masked man ordered everyone down on the floor. The gunmen looked around as if they were looking for a specific person. Zachary spotted Antoine and his boss near the rear exit. He felt that his boss was the target of this raid because he made remarks against the country's dictator.

Zachary, highly skilled in the art of ambush, formulated a plan to give cover to Antoine and his boss so that they could escape through the back exit to their waiting vehicle. Zachary knew it was a high risk, but risk came with the job. Zachary and Antoine had worked years together and build up a relationship deeper than just employees. They had a sincere love for one another. Zachary considered their boss family and didn't think twice about making the next move. He gave Antoine the single to make a run for it. On the count of three, he fired a round towards the three gunmen, hitting one of them. They all exited the club, and on Zachary's way out, he was shot in the side with one of the bullets. Antoine told the driver to take his boss back to his secure office building and went back to check on Zachary.

Antoine summoned another cab and put Zachary in it. He told the driver to drop them off at Umoja Estate, the home of Jade, a friend of Zachary's since childhood. Jade had met Zachary when he saved her life from being raped and potentially murdered by a gang that was terrifying her neighborhood. Since that day, they had been terrific friends, but she had always wanted more. After Zachary explained to her his sexual preference, she ceased her advances and understood.

91

Zachary was always welcome to her house and had his classified mail sent there for safekeeping. Her home was Zachary's safe haven.

Jade ran to get the first aid kit then examined Zachary's wound. She explained it was only a flesh wound; Antoine was relieved. For a long time, they had not taken advantage of the sexual attraction between them and had concentrated on work. Antoine took Zachary's slim-fitting polo shirt off to massage around the affected area. Antoine looked into Zachary's eyes as he tended the wound.

Zachary asked, "How are you feeling?"

He answered back with a smile and said, "Thanks for taking care of me."

Zachary's face had a particularly beautifully defying jawline. His white teeth and piercing eyes ignited an electric current through Antoine's loving system.

Zachary and Antoine had experienced sexual pleasure many times before. But on this particular night, there was something magical that happened. Nothing like the nights before. Zachary wrapped his arms around Antoine's neck, pulled in close to him, and planted a kiss on his cheek. At that moment, Antoine's wound didn't hurt. Zachary pleasured Antoine with loving kisses from his nose to his toes.

It was a night of unbelievable sexual exploration that involved all the tribal sex that could be had or imagined in the reader's mind. Their hopes, dreams and desires from this moment forward were to secure a position with King as the last ghost in his cartel.

A couple of days later, Antoine and Zachary called Jaali and asked him what the decision was about the assignment of the last cartel members.

Jaali said, "I'm still reluctant to disappoint my former employer. That is my only concern."

King informed Jaali, "In two days, four members of my Jamaican cartel will arrive in Nairobi to support Joseph and Zane in their executive service to your former employer. Now he will have six security guards in service at all times. Triple the guards that he had before. When my cartel members arrive in Nairobi, David will arrange for Antoine and Zachary to join us aboard the Tito V."

The last members of the ghost cartel arrived aboard the Tito V while it was cruising in the waters off Western New Guinea. When Antoine and Zachary stepped out of the helicopter, Assir and Jaali met them on the flight deck. All four of them embraced as old friends and proceeded to the man cave to meet King and David. Their portfolios didn't even begin to describe their handsome structures. David was taken aback by their sheer beauty. King was astounded by their grace and invited them to have a seat. The chief steward was there to take cocktail orders.

King said, "Tell us a little about yourself?"

Antoine replied, "Where does the story begin?"

Zachary broke in. "Now that we're out of Kenya, let the truth be told. Antoine and I have been lovers for over a decade. We have managed for all of these years to keep our relationship hidden by playing soccer together as youth and conducting various missions as bodyguards for the wealthy and famous in Kenya."

Their love for one another could be seen in their eyes. The passion goes without question. They would put their life on the line for one another or the cartel without question. And so, King asked them to join them, and they replied that they would be honored to be the last ghosts in the new cartel. King and David welcomed them to the Tito V and told them to check into Master Suite 5 and get cleaned up for dinner at 7 PM tonight. At which time you will be able to meet all the members of the *"Ghost Cartel."*

Zachary and Antoine entered their master suite. Stunning as it was, it did not overshadow their love for a second. They stripped down to their natural beauty of tribal men, jumped in the shower, and soaped up every crack and crevice there was. They kissed so long and lovingly they thought the shower would never end. Once they reached that queen-size bed, Antoine laid on top of Zachary and said, "Tonight is our night just reserved for ourselves. We made it, the long trip from Kenya to the South Pacific and the new cartel."

Antoine said, "Zachary, I am at your mercy. Please take care of me tonight, so ravish me."

That's exactly what Zachary did. Without even a thought in mind, he used every tribal instinct that he had to make Antoine's screams and yells of pleasure that could be heard down the entire hallway of the "Ghost Ship."

DINNER AT 7 PM

The dining room aboard the Tito V is extraordinary. The table is made of dark mahogany surrounded by chairs of the same wood, padding in white silk with **Tito V** embroidered on each chair back. The massive table stretches the yacht's full beam, the table's width being 5', allowing for two people to sit at each end and nine place settings along each side of the table. A total of 22 people may be served at one time. The galley (kitchen) is so large that it can accommodate two chefs and four sous' chefs. Meal preparation is systematically overseen by Jeff, the Executive Chef of the Tito V.

Tonight, they will have an extravagant dinner of roast lamb with mint jelly, sweet potatoes with caramel sauce and sautéed asparagus spears. Ice cream, which is a rare commodity, will be served for dessert. The newly formed "ghost cartel" will meet each other *officially* for the first time. The dress attire for the evening was native casual. Each member will describe what assets they bring to the cartel and a brief history of their relationship with their partner. Also introduced will be the Captains for all the yachts anchored at the five Islands selected for the ghost cartel. After dinner, island assignments will be negotiated and assigned among the cartel couples.

At 6:45 PM, King and David walked into the dining room and took their seat, at the head of the table, on the port side. They requested their customary drinks from the steward and adjusted their chairs so they could face one another.

David said, "This is going to be an interesting night. It is the first time we've had our ghost together to enjoy a meal and possibly each other. Let's see how their social interaction skills are tonight."

King laughed and said, "I am more interested in their social skills after dinner."

David laughed, and their drinks arrived.

King and David looked across the ship at the starboard side doorway as Assir and Jaali walked in. *What an exotic pair of killers*, King thought as they walked across the ship and took their seats at the starboard end of the table. King was reminded of the times he used his looks to kill and fade into the night.

David spoke up, "How are the leaders of the "ghost cartel" tonight?"

Assir replied, "In fact, I'm a little nervous. This is like the other side of the sword."

With his long dreadlocks perfectly braided flowing down to his chest, Jaali said, "We'll just conduct this meeting as we do before any job we pull off with our gang. I think we're more curious to see how all of them are going to interact with each other."

Assir said, "We are in a unique situation. None of us have lived in an openly gay environment. Learning to be openly gay within ourselves is our first challenge. And then living among the rest of the environment as a gay person is our next challenge. Then understanding that Jaali and I have the ultimate power and authority over a designated area of the cartel. We know major changes are affecting us daily. And I'm sure these changes are affecting every member of every team that has joined us."

King took on the challenge. "Assir, I agree with you in some ways. *Faith and family values* run strong within various religions and cultures in your country. But in the heart of a gay man, discovering oneself will happen when they trust another person, so they can grow to know themselves. My cutthroat cartel has numerous gay men, and most are couples. My question is, why is that in such a macho environment? Maybe we can toss that question around the table tonight. We will have the elite of the elite with us, and we can hear from them directly how the questions affect their masculinity."

That question was agreed upon.

Tony and Marc walked into the room dressed in Maasai tribe attire. The colors were overwhelming. Coupled with their tall tribal shield and lance, they stood out as icons in the group. Tony was a native of the Maasai tribe, which are well known for their unique culture and tribal dress. Maasai are known as a nomadic ethnic group inhabiting northern, central, and southern Kenya. Cattle herding is the main activity, and cattle are central to their lifestyle. Their diet consists of raw meat, bread, blood, and milk.

Tony put his arm around Marc's neck and said, "We are sure looking forward to dinner tonight. Having this ghost get-together is something that Marc and I have been looking forward to."

King said, "Well, let's see what the night brings!"

Ian and Cyprian were the first candidates to have been selected for the security service detail of the new cartel. They had traveled by boat, helicopter, and plane to get to the South Pacific to join King and David's security operation. Their personality, looks, and communication skills were highly polished and made them effective in the New Zealand financial market. Either one of them could persuade almost anyone to the bed chamber. They both were in a monogamous relationship since they met years ago. Monogamous, meaning if both joined in on one or two, it would be considered okay.

Two handsome men in the loincloth came in. Those were the two fishermen, Mbinga and Kaikai, from the Lake Lolwe region of Kenya. Mbinga, using his deep prismatic voice, said, "Hello everyone, this is my partner Kalkai, and he is a Tasmanian man."

Their loincloths were so skimpy and tight. Their bulges so big all eyes were on deck as they proceeded to their chairs at the table.

Mbinga said, "We are both honored to be among the ghost on this luxurious yacht."

Assir replied, "Your physical beauty is charmingly masculine. As residents on one of the chosen islands, that will be of great value. Be patient, enjoy dinner, and time will take its course."

From the port and starboard doorway, four figures arrived. Lankenua and Jamal appeared on the port side and Antoine and Zachary on starboard. Jamal pulled the chair out so that Lankenua would be seated. Then he introduced himself and his partner to the group and took a seat alongside him at the table. Antoine and Zachary came in on the other side of the table, and each introduced themselves. As they were the last couple selected to fill the cartel positions, they felt honored to be members at the table.

Then Captain Oliver of the Tito V led in and introduced the six captains of the yachts:

Frank – 200' – Tito XI New Zealand
Carl – 175'- Tito X Fiji
Laddie – 150' – Tito VIIII NEW Guinea
Tommy – 200' – Tito VIII Samoa
Phil – 175' – Tito VII New Caledonia
Captain John – 150' Tito VI Tonga Headquarters

When everyone was seated at the dining room table, there was an empty spot. Just at that moment, they could hear the helicopter approaching the yacht. They all got up and looked out the dining room window overlooking the stern where the flight deck was located. Out jumped Winston from the "Thunder Boys," San Diego's finest invisible gang. Everyone took a seat as David headed down to the flight deck to welcome him on board. Winston had previously mentioned that he wanted to volunteer his services to King and David's cartel. Tonight, he was invited as a special guest to the first dinner of the new ghost cartel.

David introduced Winston around the table and explained that his cartel provided them personal service in San Diego while they were there on a brief stop. The entire crew of the ghost ship was utilized as servers for dinner that night. Dinner service went off systematically, and Chef Jeffrey gloated once again at his culinary delight. Dinner lasted approximately 2 ½ hours. After dinner, drinks were served in the main salon and where the guests were getting intoxicated, one by one. They weren't intoxicated to a sloppy drunk, just a flighty high. They ran rapidly throughout the entire bottom deck of the ship from stateroom to stateroom, their legs spread apart by random partners. The next morning, they found themselves mostly in other ghost's quarters. Without an expression or an *excuse me, please*, everyone went back to their rooms and cleaned up for their workday ahead.

ISLAND ASSIGNMENTS

*K*ing called a mandatory meeting in which everyone had to attend. He reminded them that they did not conclude their work from the previous night -- island assignments needed to be made.

"Do any of you have a particular interest in a particular island?"

Handsome Ian and Cyprian's are talented both in the streets and in bed were best suited for New Zealand, the moneyed island. It was the most connected to the United Kingdom and its way of life. They both felt comfortable that they could blend into the island's high-end lifestyle and effectively establish a network needed to identify and cut off the drug shipments coming into their country. Ian and Cyprian joined Captain Frank at the helm and left for New Zealand the following morning for a small river port by the name of Gisborne. The Tito 200' XI draft was only 8' so it could navigate comfortably all of the ports along the river, where larger ships could not go.

Fiji was the best match for Jamal and Lankenua. Lankenua was educated, and Jamal was from a wealthy family on the East Coast of Kenya. They had been together for over 10 years and served at the highest level in executive service to tribal chiefs. They were both an exceptionally handsome couple that could freeze one's eyes when they were looked upon. They fit the perfect mold of the ghost cartel. Love them, enjoy them, and all will be lost. Along with Captain Carl and the 175' Tito X and crew, they sailed off to Fiji from the waters of Western New Zealand, where they been cruising this last week or two.

New Caledonia is an ideal assignment for Antoine and Zachary. It is the largest of the French overseas islands in the South Pacific. Its capital territory is Noumea which is extremely modern, and the island's total landmass is 7170 mi.^{2}. Many people of African descent are the majority of the rich people in the Southern Province where the 175' Tito VII, captained by Phil, will be docked.

The Samoan islands are noted for their fishing and secluded islands that could capitalize on the drug trade. Mbinga and Kaikai grew up on fishing vessels and served on a service detail for a large fishing fleet boss. They were comfortable around sweaty fishermen that it takes to manage the catch, and they are slick enough to keep a low profile while searching for the cartel leaders on the islands. They boarded the 200' Tito VIII with Captain Tommy, navigating name them to the port of Apia, on the northern end of Upolu Island, which is the only major port in Samoa.

Tony and Mark were assigned to New Guinea. It was the last island available. They both had an excellent reputation in executive service. New Guinea's thriving business culture will use their talents to infiltrate the new financial districts that are now popping up on the largest island in the southern hemisphere. New Guinea is divided into two districts, West Papua and Papua, their capitals Manokwari and Jayapura, respectively. Many of the islands still have tribal warfare. Large areas of New Guinea have yet to be explored by scientists and archaeologists, leaving a large area for the drug business to be established. One of the dangers to look out for a New Guinea are its crocodiles, mainly in the uninhabited island areas. Captain Laddie and the Tito VIIII, the 150' yacht, are now heading for Papua New Guinea, one of its lesser-known ports.

WINSTON

A question remained as to what Winston's assignment would be. He and his affiliates served King well while he was in San Diego with his deceased lover Jim. After that, Winston had joined Jim on Marquis Island to celebrate Jim's final party before Jim passed on to another life. At this event, Winston expressed his desire to work for the Marquis Cartel. Not realizing then, what he knows now, King and David have formed a new cartel in Nuku'alofa, the capital of Tonga. They need a strong leader with a reputation that gets the job done. That person is going to be Winston and his "Thunder Boys." They will be charged with managing the operation center in Tonga, where all the drugs will be cut and redistributed to various smaller cartels in the South Pacific.

Winston, a strikingly handsome man, was now alone with King in the ghost ship's office for the first time since they met. He stood 5'11" of Spanish descent, black hair, brown eyes, and a medium build. He did not stand out as cutthroat head of a cartel group. His sexual appearance was one that you would expect a Spaniard to have. His hands appeared soft and fingers long, nails manicured to reveal his delicate side. When he sat in the office next to King, his legs were spread apart, revealing a massive bulge in his tight black pants that King could not keep his eyes off of during their conversation.

Eventually, Winston stood up and walked over to King, pressed his bulge up against King's lips. Then he asked, "Would you like a taste of the nectar from the person that's going to run your operation in the Kingdom of Tonga?"

King, use to all the subtleties of sex in his cartel, reached up and unzipped the black pants revealing a massive uncut cock. When it was fully erect, he devoured it to its base. While it was in his mouth, he looked up at Winston's eyes, and Winston said, "Go for it, King, it's all yours."

After Winston delivered his sweet milk into King's mouth, King savored the taste, licked his lips, and gently zipped up Winston's pants. Winston and King embraced lovingly. King's lover, Jim, had died over two years ago. He was not searching for another to take Jim's place, but Winston would be at the top of the list if he were.

King went over all the detailed plans of the new cartel. Winston's operation in San Diego was quite similar to Kings planning for the South Pacific. Winston would obtain thousands of kilos from his Mexican connection and redistribute them to his contacts in the western United States and Canada. Over the last eight years, he had established a quiet, nondescript distribution route to handle the volume of "white powder" that came his way. The only difference in King's operation that he could see is that they would have to hijack the shipments instead of the powder being sent directly to them. Heisting the shipments could be a very dangerous event and would require the resources of everyone on hand.

King asked Winston, "How many members are in the "Thunder Boys?"

Winston replied, "25. As you know, I run a quiet and well-integrated team. We handle kilos upon kilos of powder every week through our distribution network. My entire team are skilled to avoid any encounter, blend in, and protect the shipments with their lives while in transit to our connection."

"How many of your team are you going to bring to Tonga to handle our operation?"

"How much volume do you anticipate?"

King replied, "At this time, we're uncertain as to the amount that we are going to intercept. David had done his homework as to shipments flowing into islands. Still, we have not, as of today, determined the number of shipments.

"I will start off by bringing 10 of my team, as 10 accommodations have been built at the operations center. I will stay onboard the ghost ship, and let me remind you, you can visit anytime. My team will be here in three days."

King instructed Captain Oliver to head the Tito V to the operations center in Tonga, where Winston can board his yacht and assume command.

After reaching the port, King dropped off Winston at his office in Tonga and headed out to sea in his nondescript ghost yacht. He told Captain Oliver to cruise around the many islands of Tonga, to be close by, just in case Winston needed his support. It took a while for Winston to get accustomed to the technology installed on the Tito VI. He was ill-prepared and ill-trained to use such technology. Wayne, Captain Oliver's right-hand man, took Winston under his charge and spent several days going over the advanced warning systems, armament and Winston was introduced to all the crew members on the yacht. The Tito VI was now his home, and he had never lived so lavishly in all his life.

When all this gang arrived in Tonga, Winston held a staff meeting in the Tonga conference room. His boys (or men) were anxious to understand their new operation. Winston went into detail as to King's plan. When hearing the plan, his men were jubilant. Before, they were just fetching and hauling the powder. Now they're going to steal it, deliver it and sell it. It was a whole new direction that they had not taken before. One of the boys spoke up and said, "Get your pistol loaded, boys." There was a sense of high adrenaline that flowed around the conference room. Winston was excited to see it and feel it. Because he wanted his "thunder boys" to be the pride of the ghost cartel.

GOODBYE ANDREW AND STEPHEN

Andrew and Stephen were put out to pasture. They had allowed the mutiny to originate on their watch while they managed the Tonga operation. King could not trust them with this vast operation now forming. He gave them both instructions to report back to Marquis Island immediately, as soon as Winston and his associates arrived. King called Aaron and Bryan on the secure line and then told them the story about Andrew and Stephen and the mutiny that had happened under their watch. He also told him to handle them as they wished. They had been replaced within his organization by Winston and his associates from San Diego. King nor David heard nothing more about Andrew and Stephen from that point on. Their whereabouts were unknown, and their names were not spoken any longer.

THE FIRST DRUG SEIZURE

*W*inston was sitting in the control room on the Tito VI. The radar system alerted that a freighter was approaching the island of Nauru, which is the smallest island in the Oceana group of islands in the South Pacific. Winston's research revealed no port on the island to offload cargo, and it was over a thousand nautical miles to any larger port authority. He found that completely strange and placed a secure call to Jaali, the ghost leader, and informed him of his findings.

Jaali and Assir consulted with Captain Oliver, pulling out all the charts and referring to the GPS system. Their research revealed that the cargo ship originated from Columbia. They looked at each other and said, 'It's probably full of Colombian gold." Winston got on the phone with one of his "boys" that he left behind in San Diego. He told them to ask their Mexican contact what Columbia is shipping to the South Pacific. It only took two hours for a return phone call to come in on the secure line announcing that this ship is used continuously for drug shipments. The freighter generally anchors out at the island of Talau, in the kingdom of Tonga. It is one of the northern islands with very few inhabitants. King was told that a plan was now being formulated to offload all the white powder and send it to the Tonga operation center for further distribution.

Now realizing that Talau is the distribution point for the "Colombian Gold," Assir and Jaali have an opportunity to prove to King and David that they can once again plan and execute some "black magic." They will get its many kilos into the Tonga operation center before the cargo ship reaches Tonga's shore. All six ghost ships could load their fast boats by using their cranes and place them on the pool area covered with teak decking. Also, onboard each yacht are two short boats. Jaali gave Captain Oliver instructions to have all captains plot a course for the island of Talau. The container ship carrying the "Colombian Gold" is approximately 1900 miles away from Tonga, with a cruise speed of 9 kn. The average cruising speed of all the ghost ships is 10 kn. Meaning from any location in the South Pacific, the ghost cartel should be able to intercept the "Colombian Gold" before it reaches its intended port.

The freighter didn't know what was happening. It could identify, on its radar, six vessels floating in proximity to their planned course of sailing to the island of Talau. Never before had they ever picked up, maybe but one or two vessels, on their radar while delivering its cargo in the South Pacific. When they came within 50 miles of their delivery point, 12 "go boats," black in color and very difficult to distinguish during the nighttime, began encircling their ship. Over the loudspeaker system, the container ship could hear the warning to "stop and prepare for boarding." That message alerted the container ship's captain, and they went into full protective action.

The container ship was only staffed with 20 people, including the captain, first officer and engineers. The fighting force of the container ship was meager at best. The ship captain knew nothing of its cargo other than they needed to stop at Talau Island to offload a shipment before pressing on to the next port. When the container ship was dead in the water, two of the "go boats" pulled up alongside, and 10 cartel members boarded the ship. The staff on the container ship did not resist and complied with all verbal requests. The leader of the cartel group requested the ship's manifest, which indicated that the "Colombian Gold" was stored in the grain holding areas in the bottom of the freighter. After a review, it was revealed that they were wrapped and netted, ready to be removed easily upon docking. The total weight of the shipment was 10 bundles weighing 1,000 pounds each, netted and ready to be unloaded from the freighter while in port. The group leader had the crane operator on board the freighter transfer one bundle to a "go boat" for inspection. When it was opened by the crew, they were shocked when it was revealed that each netted bundle contained over 445 kilos of white powder. Estimating the total hall at approximately 4,545 kilos. 1 kg had an estimated resale value of USD 15,000. Their first seizure totaled over USD 68,175,000.00—a direct profit to the bottom line.

Their smaller craft carried the product back to the ghost ship in which they loaded into the storage area that was formally the pool, and each yacht headed for Tonga. One by one, they pulled into the dock at the Tonga headquarters, where netted bags of cargo were transferred from the vessel to the warehouse. Then they were cut into smaller and more manageable loads to be sold to small cartels throughout the South Pacific at $5,000 per kilo, below the current going rate. The crew of the freighter and all affected by this operation had no clue what was going on. The freighter continued on its course delivering its cargo to other ports in the South Pacific.

Even at the discounted rate, the proceeds were more than needed for operating costs that the ghost cartel required to sustain its operation. This one hit alone covered their operating cost for the first year's startup and left them with a healthy bank account. Jaali and Assir now understood the quickness of their operation to secure white powder and how to disseminate it. He instructed each Captain to monitor the radar and watch out for freighters coming into their area of responsibility from foreign locations. Winston should be consulted about drug movements from the other parts of the world, and no attempt to secure the vessel should be overlooked. After their successful mission, Jaali and Assir retired to their private quarters and made more tribal love. Jaali led the way just as he did the day of the "cut," when his manly spear was on display for Assir to adore while it healed. Once healed, Assir had been pleased by it, every day in every way.

4545 KILOS OF WHITE POWDER

One by one, the ghost ships dropped off their haul at the operations center in Tonga. Winston's men cut down each kilo into manageable bundles. They loaded them on the "go boats" standing by at the dock to be delivered throughout the small ports in the Kingdom of Tonga.

Each ghost ship stood by as their white powder was cut and reloaded on their ship to be resold on the small islands of Oceana in the South Pacific. As each Captain pulled into their future port of operation, they and their assigned leaders assessed the risk of each sale. The smaller cartels who bought powder were local and very unorganized. They were grateful for the product's low price, creating an extra profit they will now be making.

Winston staffed the Tonga operations center with 10 of his men from San Diego. They were exceptionally good-looking men. His operation in San Diego blended into all environments where they delivered the product. Each member of his operation reflected a different cultural and ethnic background. They were trained to operate independently and had amazing self-confidence. Winston was a magnificent low-profile leader of the group. He did not get involved in his members' sexual exploits, and they did not get involved with his.

Winston had not had a close relationship with another individual for a long time. His primary focus was on his business to ensure that he pleased his Mexican contacts and that all of the powder was distributed as agreed in a timely manner. Over the last eight years, his group had made millions of dollars. They all lived a comfortable lifestyle. It had been on only rare occasions that the DEA, FBI, or any other authority detected their silent operation. They enjoyed being invisible.

As the ghost ships unloaded their first load of powder, they went back to their port assignments. The captains and island managers assessed the success of their operation. They knew that another mission would be announced any day, and they had to stand ready to make it as successful as the first. Each island manager was hoping that they were the one to head up the next mission.

KING AND WINSTON

After King and David finished dinner on the Tito V, King excused himself and slowly took a trip around the yacht, enjoying the beautiful sunset, in a feeling of total loneliness. He was wondering how much longer he could stand this loneliness. He valued David's love, but it was not emotionally fulfilling. Despite his age, his strong sexual urges needed to be satisfied. Since losing Jim, no one had been able to do that.

As he was sitting alone on the upper sundeck, he asked the steward to bring him a scotch and soda, then he reclined on the lounge chair. Looking up at the stars, he ran his fingers down his neck, over his erect nipples, down his washboard abs to his Jamaican cock and masturbated. As he was masturbating, his drink arrived. The steward pretended he didn't see a thing and went on his merry way. King closed his eyes and continued his mighty strokes on the harder than normal, uncut manhood. When the immense gusher flowed all over himself from his T-shirt to his deck pants, King realized he was thinking of Winston. This magical Spanish man came into his life by accident and now has a grip on him mentally, emotionally, and sexually.

What am I going to do?

King called Captain Oliver, requesting the location of the Tito V. Captain Oliver told him that they were 10 hours west of the capital of Tonga. He asked Captain Oliver to call the Captain John of the Tito VI and charter a course to meet them halfway between their two points. King then called Winston and asked him if he would enjoy meeting him within the next five hours for a rendezvous. Winston was overjoyed and surprised. King informed him that he had already told the captain of his yacht to head his way, and they would rendezvous shortly.

Winston jumped in the shower. He slowly cleansed all his body cavities and his long Spanish tool, hoping that he would use it, or his own ass would be used within hours by the notorious King of the Jamaican Cartel. King's reputation is so well-known throughout the cartel world that Winston felt privileged to be at his side. Whatever the case may be, being under or over him would be a dream that few people will enjoy.

Both yachts anchored off the secluded island. Winston's "shore boat" delivered him to the Tito V, and King welcomed him on board. They both retreated to the game room on the upper deck and enjoyed a round of mimosas to get their juices flowing. Winston was sitting on the sofa and King on the chair across from them. Winston watched as King got up out of his chair and walked around behind the sofa and began massaging his neck and shoulders.

Winston put his head back and looked up at King's eyes and said, "With your strong Jamaican fingers, you're making me tingle all the way down to my toes."

King replied, "Is that all I make tingle?"

Winston grabbed both of King's hands and began to kiss them, finger by finger. King had not felt this aroused by another man since his lover Jim. His body was aching for affection.

Winston got up and faced King within inches. When he did, King grabbed Winston by the neck, threw him back on the sofa, and begin to smother him with those infectious Jamaican kisses. Winston's Spanish adrenaline hit the boiling point. He wanted nothing more than to have King take him as his slave tonight, but that was not what King had planned. He rolled Winston over on top of him. He pulled off his shirt, which revealed a smooth Spanish body with slightly hairy armpits and protruding nipples begging to be sucked. King went to work on them immediately. He licked his smooth stomach down to his navel, encircling it, filled it full of spit, and then sucked it dry. Winston was still wearing those tight black pants, which King hastily removed them from his body. Winston flipped King over on his back and removed his shirt that revealed his six-pack chest and Jamaican bulge in his pants.

Together they got up, took a final swig of their mimosas, and headed off to King's master suite on the upper level of the yacht. Once inside, it was like a game of cat and mouse. Winston and King never stopped exploring each other's bodies until they found the exact moment when Winston's 9" Spanish dick buried its way into King's manhole. King knew what he wanted from the very start -- to be dominated by this luscious Spaniard. He pushed himself smoothly on Winston's cock without a groan or moan. His pleasure was so instant that he could not even imagine that Winston had been in his life all this time, and today he felt like King of the Cartel once again.

King and Winston spent two days anchored together off the small island in the South Pacific.

Winston was 12 years younger than King and had never shared his life with another man. He had kept his personal life low profile within his criminal organization. King was well known for having Jim as his companion until his demise over two years ago. Since he and David's establishment of the ghost cartel, he recognized the value of having another dominant figure in his life. Even though Winston was so much younger, he was the perfect companion. They were both masterminds in crime. And they were both accomplished in bringing sexual pleasure to their partners, which is necessary to keep their personality, looks, and communication skills polished. Happiness brings prosperity, and prosperity is an attribute of love. King and Winston were now in the infancy of love.

CAIN AND ABEL

$\mathcal{K}$ing and David were relaxing in the upper deck game room when Jaali and Assir walked in. King asked them to sit down and relax. Assir went to the wet bar and made him and his partner a drink. Assir began talking about the story he was told when he was a child growing up in his village. His grandfather had told him this incredible story about Cain and Abel, two brothers. One a shepherd, and the other was a farmer. They were nomads in the tribal area of Kenya and were dedicated to one another. Their mother of unknown origin breastfed them until they were 6 years old, making them the oldest of the tribal children breastfed in the region. As a result, all the people noticed their tall, bony structure, mainly because of the unusually bright-colored skuas they wore. Cain was dark as a black falcon, and Abel just a bit shorter and full of emotion like a woman. Assir said his grandfather told him that the stories were probably a myth. Still, they were so interesting that he could not resist telling the exotic details these two characters exhibited in the tribal area where they existed.

It was rumored in this story that their mother favored one over the other. Each brother did everything they could to impress their mother and to hide their love for one another. While maturing, everyone grew suspicious of their closeness they shared. When they graduated from middle school, Cain's parents caught them having sex in the small sleeping room attached to Cain's hut. This one act alone sealed both of their fates with their family's fortune. So now, ostracized by their families, they were sent to boarding school.

It was said that when they were in boarding school, Cain would still follow Abel like a black falcon everywhere he went. They even bunked together in the same dormitory during the four years they spent in high school, one bunk on the top the other on the bottom. They often shared intimate moments in the shower behind the dormitory in the late hours of the night. Cain masterfully took charge of Abel's feminine body every chance he got. As they matured into young adults, they were inseparable even though everyone knew their situation. It was said that Lucifer watched over them and protected them from the onslaught of verbal and physical abuse. Then one day, a very brave but stupid classmate viciously raped Abel in the back of a deserted classroom. When Cain stepped in, at the stroke of midnight, he dragged the rapist down the hallway, grabbed the unnamed individual by the back of his head and slit his throat. He stood there watching while the rapist bled to death.

When Cain asked Lucifer for forgiveness, Lucifer said, "No problem, you made the right decision. In fact, I planted the seed in your mind for the action you took tonight."

Revenging Abel's vulgar ass pounding is just a myth, as the legend goes. That was the first time Lucifer saved King's life when he was 12 years old.

It was King who Lucifer saved that night, and it was not a myth. King has lived at the right hand of Lucifer, who is now telling the story of King, David, and their ghost cartel, while they navigate to Nendo Island to host a surprise birthday party for the King among kings and the disciples of the "ghost cartel."

JULY 6th – PLANNING

*D*avid was sitting in the man cave on the Tito V. He put in a call to Oliver to join him. When Oliver came into the room, David asked him to sit down and offered him a drink which he declined.

David said, "Oliver, we have a big party to plan. It's King's 51st birthday on July 6, and this is the first day birthday that he has ever celebrated since I have known him, and I want to make it a big splash.

"I have studied the charts and selected the Santa Cruz Islands, which are located 250 miles southeast of the Samoan Islands, as an ideal location for the big bash. Its largest island is Nendo, which has about 5000 people, small enough but big enough to supply us with the necessary food and beverage for the party. We can summon all our yachts and staff to that location and anchor on the deserted side of the island. We will commandeer the mile-long beach as our playground."

Captain Oliver was familiar with the island as he had sailed there before. He asked David, "Is this going to be a surprise party or what, and if he was going to share the planning with King?"

David replied, "No, it's a big surprise. Send out a broadcast to the other captains of the yachts to charter a course for Nendo Island so that we all arrived simultaneously around July 4th. Also, when you broadcast the message, have them restock their pantries just in case the supplies on the small island are limited."

After Captain Oliver departed to go to the yacht bridge, David placed a call for Assir and Jaali to join him in the office in the man cave. When they arrived, he told them that he wanted to have a conversation with them about a party he was planning to have. He wanted all the details to be confidential. They were extremely excited to find out who the party was for because such secrecy was uncommon aboard the Tito V. David continued to explain that Captain Oliver would send instructions for all captains to charter a course for their yachts to the small remote island of Nendo, about 2000 miles from where they were currently located.

Jaali, the fearless one, asked, "Who are we throwing this party for?"

With the biggest smile on his face, David replied, "It's King's 51st birthday, and will he ever be surprised. Never since I have known him has he celebrated his birthday. He avoids that special day like the plague because he knows that on each passing day, he's getting older. He fears the time will come that he will not be able to perform the two things that are important in his life – being the master of this cutthroat cartel and master in the bed chamber. King has led a charmed life, guarded by Lucifer, as he slipped in and out of sight for years. He has fulfilled every sexual fantasy that a person could enjoy. Lucifer has protected him in every battle, big or small. Captain Oliver told David that their trip to Nendo island at their cruising speed of 10 kn would take approximately a week. During this time, the crew will have time to give the yacht a once-over cleaning and take a long-deserved rest after their first $68 million heist.

The detailed planning for the party was almost overwhelming David. He called upon his loyal right-hand men, Jaali and Assir, to help him with some of the details. All seven yachts of the cartel will be anchored off of Nendo Island, and every security precaution had to be taken. David assigned that task to Simon. Never before in their South Pacific operation had all of the ghost ships of the cartel operation been in one location at any given point in time. Detailed security planning for this part of the operation was an important element to the party's success. Simon put a call into GYS security in Miami. He requested 20 mercenaries to be dispatched by private jet to the island that will host the party.

You only can imagine this two-mile-long white sandy beach. In its harbor, there are anchored six black and silver yachts looking almost identical except their size, glistening in the night, housing the entire staff and crew and leaders of the "Ghost Cartel,"

David instructed Captain Oliver to cruise slowly to the party destination. He wanted Captain Oliver to anchor at the north end of the Nendo Island. This way, King would not notice the crowded yachts of the cartel gathered around the beach where the party would be held. The detailed planning for the event started to cross David's desk. Chef Jeffrey headed up all of the food supply supported by the smaller yachts. Those preparations were well underway. The Chief Steward was in charge of all alcohol, mixers, and a broad range of soft drinks and ice. The deckhands, who numbered about 18, were responsible for beach huts, chairs, and paraphernalia. Of course, all the drugs that you could ever possibly want would be there by the truckload to be enjoyed.

Simon was the last person to finish his security checklist. When he ran the island's name by GYS as security in Miami, he found a glitch. Apparently, the island had a tie to a small Mafia cartel that handled the imported drugs, then cut and shipped to the smaller islands in the Samoan chain. Simon summoned Mbinga and Kaikai (the island's Kenyan Men) to the mancave.

"Did you know your island has a small cartel?"

"No, what did your inquiry reveal?"

"I don't know where the drugs came from, but they were cut by this small cartel and further distributed throughout the Samoan Islands, which will be your clients someday."

Simon informed David about the information he received on the Samoan cartel. And that the Kenyan men that had been assigned there had not yet discovered its operation.

David asked, "Do you think we can hold the party, get in and out of the island within a few days, undetected?"

"I doubt it. David, you already alerted our arrival by the large orders of food and booze to be delivered to the beach on the island's east side. Since the town on this island has only 5,000 people, I am sure by now everybody knows what's going on."

"Simon, what should I do?"

"I suggest you use your Kenyan men along with my mercenaries who are flying in. That will give us a total number of 23 well-armed men. We can infiltrate this small island and identify the cartel members quickly, then execute them. Sooner or later, we will have to do it anyway."

David replied, "That's a decision that King usually makes."

"David, it's time for you to make a hard decision if you want to keep King's birthday a secret."

"Okay, run the mission. I don't want to hear about the gory details other than it was completed."

Now with that problem solved, the ghost ships were starting to arrive under cover of darkness. One by one, they anchored in the bay on the east side of the island. Their shore boats were cruising between yachts, and the crewmembers were exchanging love with one another that they had not shared for months. They were so happy to be back together, minutes turned into hours, and unfortunately, daybreak arose. Exhausted from a night of turbulence between staterooms and bunks, they all showered off the male stench of love from the night before. They were ready to serve their masters of the ship with respect until the day was complete and back to bed to enjoy sex between the sheets again.

The night before the party, while Oliver was cruising the yacht towards its final destination. Winston, the Black Falcon, as King referred to him, was thinking about King whom he had just made love to only the night before. He was fascinated by this handsome Puerto Rican man. King had such power and control of hundreds upon hundreds of cutthroat men in several cartels with his autocratic authority, like a kingdom of his own. At the same time, Winston further fantasized about dominating King like a little girl in bed. Winston's massive Black Falcon body, so dark and so lean, could spear him from across the room and make him beg for more pleasuring with just a stare. He visualized King down on his hands and knees, crawling towards him to worship his big spear hanging between his legs to put his lips around it and milk it dry.

BIRTHDAY PARTY – JULY 6th

*A*ll the yachts except the 250' Tito V were anchored in the cluster at the east side of the alignment. Their shore boats had transported all but their captains to the beach for King's big birthday celebration. David had arranged for a huge firework celebration to be kicked off at 10 PM. At that time, the shore boats from the Tito V, which could carry 20 staff and crew to the celebration, were scheduled to arrive at the island. Captain Oliver and his first mate Wayne were ready to lower the boats into the water when gunfire erupted. Captain Oliver sounded the alarm, and everyone reported to their respective duty stations fully armed. On his radar, he could observe 20 to 25 smaller craft surrounding the six yachts anchored off the eastern side of the island.

Captain Oliver radioed Simon on the island and informed him that they were being attacked by an unknown number of armed personnel. Captain Oliver told King of the attack, and King asked, "Why all of our cartel yachts anchored off the eastern side of the island?"

David spoke up, "King, today is your birthday, and I was going to have a surprise party for you. I guess it's going to be a different party than the planned."

"David, I love your dearly, but you have exposed our entire ghost cartel to a takeover operation by an unknown enemy."

King got on the phone and ordered the 20 mercenaries to board four of the shore boats and head out to cut off the smaller crafts proceeding to attack the six yachts. One by one, the mercenary shore boats were plucked off. The remaining staff and crew boarded the shore boats and made it back to their yachts and began fortifying them with high-powered weapons to defend themselves. The captains powered up the yachts and attempted to power away to the open sea; the Tito VIII & Tito VII sustained major damage. They were idling dead in the water when they were boarded by 10 of the smaller craft—the staffing crew engaged in a bloodbath battle, until they secured their yachts. The remainder of the cartel yachts managed to escape to the open sea. Eight members of the ghost cartel were killed, and all the 10 smaller craft were executed during the fight, but the remaining smaller craft fled the fight.

By the time King's birthday was over, his ghost cartel had taken a major hit. Two of his ghost ships sustained significant damage. They were idling helplessly east of Nendo Island, and the remainder were heading back to their designated ports. The 250' Tito V, anchored north of the island, had gone undetected during the raid. It motored east to assess the two yachts that had sustained damage. The engineers and crew of the yachts combined worked endlessly to repair the damage. In the end, the two damaged boats limped back to their ports for much needed repairs.

The ghost cartel had taken quite a hit -- from whom King wanted to know. *How did this happen to us?* He asked David about the planning process for this party and who was involved. King's concern was that how this small island of 5000 people could do this much damage to the big ghost cartel.

"How in the hell could this happen? There's either a rat among us or on the island, and we have to find out who it is. Or was it the small cartel that we partially eliminated earlier?" Simon's research had revealed that this small cartel's operation was not that threatening.

King summoned the Black Falcon to his suite. He needed to be ravaged like a bitch in heat. He needed to understand how anyone could dominate his cartel, and the only way he knew how to do it was to be dominated himself. After the Falcon ravaged him for hours, he was energized to think through the mess. He studied all the contacts and suspected that it was the food vendor for the party on the beach that had disclosed their location. King took Winston, Assir and Jaali into town and looked up the caterer who supplied the food.

After they grabbed him and took him to the Tito V, they put his nuts in a vice grip until he admitted leaking their location to the head of the small local cartel who arranged for the raid on their beach party. After his admission, King took him to the operating room in the lower area level of the yacht and castrated him like a boar and threw his nuts overboard along with his body parts to chum the sharks and not to be seen anymore.

King, now 51 years old, had survived yet another cartel attack. He told Captain Oliver to head the Tito V to a disclosed location in the South Pacific so that he and his crew could recuperate from the attack. He placed a call to all of his ghost cartel leaders and requested them to arrange for helicopter transport to the Tito V for a meeting. Firm plans need to be made so this event never happens again. No matter who arranges a party or a gathering, under no circumstances will the yachts be in one location together again. All of the Kenyan men will gather as "Knights of the Roundtable" to secure the future of the "Ghost Cartel".

A KENYA MAN

Muscles strong, shoulders wide,
below his brows lie to windows open deep,
tell tales of a tall warrior and a
heart ready to love, fingers are ready to pull the trigger,
his majestic smile,
a gap widened between his lower teeth,
reveal hands vile, skin dipped in melanin fine as wine.
Swift as a gazelle, claws ready to pounce on prey,
his commanding presence, arresting eyes
like a phoenix, ready to conquer, ready to rise,
through his veins flow fire and loyalty,
woe unto him who gets in his way.

By Antony

A KENYA BOY

Brave Kenyan boys
at the age of 15 are sent off to
the forest to complete the ritual of "tumin" while the
cut heals
they are surrounded and adorned by hundreds of
young men
dancing naked
to heal and hear fables from their elders. It's during
this time
that the "black magic" begins to attract oneself to
"A Kenya Man."

By Antony

LUCIFER GOES ON TO SAY...

Lucifer says the fascinating part about this journey that we're on is that we look through my eyes as to "The corruption, killing, lovemaking and sex between the cartel members of King's cutthroat gang." All of these corrupt actions have made for great stories. Today's leaders in King's cartel are from Kenya, where men are proud to be *Kenyan men*.

As Lucifer, I sincerely hope that I bring forth to you the beauty, intelligence, grace and swiftness of Kenyan men who staff our newly formed ghost cartel. They are not shy but brave. They are sexy to a fault. Over a period of time, each team will establish a base of operation on a South Pacific island. Some more successful than others. The "ghost cartel's" success may be defined by only one shipment of drugs that is so large that it can finance the cartel's operation for a year.

All of these planned attacks come with high risk. All will be revealed in the chapters that follow."

Who is the best at strategizing and executing the plans? Do they all live to enjoy another day? As King's and David's protector, Lucifer said, "I know how all the stories end."

The following books are entitled "Ghost Cartel in New Zealand," "Ghost Cartel in New Caledonia," etc. Lucifer said, "They should be exciting reads."

To be continued...

ABOUT THE AUTHOR
James Marquis

*J*ames was born the son of sharecroppers and grew up in tenement housing on a farm in Iroquois County, Illinois. At the age of thirteen, he and his family moved to a small village in the same county where he graduated high school. At the age of seventeen, he moved from the small village to Champaign, Illinois, the home of the University of Illinois, and he secured a position as a teller at one of the major banks. Because of his "Personality, Looks and Communication Skills," it was not long before he was promoted to head teller. During this time frame, he was drafted into the Army to supplement the surge of troops during the Vietnamese crisis.

His distinguished military career was recognized when he received a Bronze Star Medal. His training in the Army prepared him to pursue his life's dream of acquiring financial freedom. After he was discharged from the Army, he returned to the small Illinois bank and discovered it had limited promotional opportunities for him to achieve his dream.

James sought out and attained a position with one of the world's largest banks based in California, where he spent twenty-five years. During this time, he worked internationally in fifteen different countries around the world. Additionally, he was recognized as the bank's top motivational speaker. After spending ten years overseas, he was invited to join the Chief Executive Officer of International Operations as his attaché. He served in that position for five years. During that time, he supervised all of the World Bank's international operation centers with the highest degree of efficiency.

Upon completing this assignment, he served for ten years as the Regional VP of Operations for Northern California. After which, he retired at the age of forty-five. Upon retirement, he spent several months on his yacht named *The Jim Marquis* until he relocated to Key West Florida. After several years he relocated to his Lakehouse in the upper Peninsula of Michigan and enjoyed the tranquility that only remoteness can provide. After a decade and tiring of the snowy cold winters, he relocated to southern Texas for a decade.

In 2019, he returned home to Sacramento, California. He chooses to reside in one of the exclusive apartments in midtown Sacramento.

While watching all the movies that television could provide during the pandemic, he wrote his first book, *1862 A Civil War Love Story*, in which he visualized "Michael B. Jordan" as the lead character. 1862 is the forbidden love story that involves Confederate soldiers, plantation workers and a couple of rednecks from Kentucky during the waning years of the civil war. Since its release, the book has received 5-star reviews. The book's writing was influenced by the storyline of *Brokeback Mountain*, a compelling interracial gay novel far exceeding the love between men as characterized in *Brokeback Mountain*.

He continued to write three books in a series of international intrigue, imprisonment, drugs, love lost and found again, success and failure, and of course, love and passion.

First in the series is *1968 A Vietnam War Love Story*, a fictional story influenced by his own personal events before, during, and after his tour of duty in Vietnam. This book goes into the emotional side of war. The main character takes you on a journey lasting two decades of love lost and found again, multibillion-dollar business decisions, high finance, international intrigue, and the love stories continue.

The next in the series is *The Marquis Cartel,* and the final book is *The Revenge of the Marquis Cartel.* All three storylines have the main characters, and their lovers accidentally stumble on the resources to form a Cartel. The leaders of the Marquis Cartel recognize they are novices at securing the safety of the members of the cartel, so they enlist the support of two notorious cutthroat gangs and mercenaries. These books are filled with drugs, passion, death, international suspense, prison, unconditional love, and of course, a gay love story or two.

After these stories were finished and published, James began work on his next series, entitled the *Ghost Cartel.* This series features a beautiful collection of Kenyan Men who were so eloquently characterized by a representative that he employed from Eldoret, Kenya. He attempted to keep these characters true to form, representing numerous tribes from Kenya. Collectively they form a large cartel in the South Pacific. James is continually challenged to create suspense, killings, sexual intrigue, and suspense while representing *A Kenyan Man*.

These novellas have brought recognition to Jim as an inspiring new author who dares to be himself.

DISCLAIMER TO THE READER

This is a work of fiction. names, characters, businesses, events and instances are the product of the author's imagination. Any resemblance to the actual persons living or dead, or actual events is purely accidental.

References: Wikipedia

www.ingramcontent.com/pod-product-compliance
Lightning Source LLC
Chambersburg PA
CBHW071306130626
46556CB00004B/1486